Camp Kachemak
Mystery

Halene Petersen Dahlstrom

D1004743

Camp Kachemak
Mystery

A Rinnie of Alaska Adventure
Book Two

Halene Petersen Dahlstrom

PO Box 221974 Anchorage, Alaska 99522-1974

ISBN 978-1-59433-065-0

Library of Congress Catalog Card Number: 2007938771

Manufactured in the United States of America

Dedication

This book is dedicated to those who believe in me,
friends, old and new,
family, kind and true,
and, Dan, especially to you.

Table of Contents

A Note from the Author

"Everyone has a story." That's what Rinnie Cumberland's mother reminds her. I was reminded of it over and over as I talked with people while researching this book. Everyone has a camp story! I endeavored to weave real-life experiences and imagination together for *Camp Kachemak Mystery*. Mud puddle volleyball games, surprises in the oatmeal pot, a troubled plane making a big splash, and a girl dealing with a tragic family past are just a few of the incidents that were based on real events. A special order purchased from the *BeJeweled by Renee* website proved that Rinnie's necklace could actually exist too.

I am very blessed to have wonderful family members and forever-dear friends who take an active interest in my writing, spare precious time to preview at various stages, and provide valuable feedback. Many thanks to you all!

My hope for this story is that people will smile, chuckle, and take away a little something extra to lighten their load, or brighten their day.

Best Wishes and Happy Reading!

Chapter 1

Friday Fright

Rinnie Cumberland was running, running, running. Her heart was pounding harder, and harder. She could barely breathe. Someone was chasing her, gaining on her. Who was it? Who? She glanced behind. Magda? Yes! It was mean, haggy Magda, who'd tried once before to catch Rinnie. It was that same ornery, scheming witch Rinnie had turned in to the police in order to save Mr. Moore. But how could it be Magda? She was in jail. Had she escaped? No way! Rinnie couldn't think straight. All she could do was run!

She could hear Magda getting closer and closer. Rinnie forced herself onward. The hill was steep. Would she ever reach the top? She had to keep going. Her eyes scanned for clues of something familiar as she ran through the branches and bushes. Where was the tree house? If she could just get up into the tree house safely, she could call for help. But it was taking forever to get there. Don't give up. Go, go!

Finally, it came into view. At first glance, Rinnie couldn't see the rope ladder. Oh no! Panicked, Rinnie tried to yell. No sound came out. Her lungs felt as if they'd split open. Noise behind her gave her one last burst of energy, and the next thing she knew, she was at the base of the tree. To her relief, the rope ladder was there after all. Reaching out to grab it, her arms felt like anchors and she struggled to lift them. You can do it. Try one at a time, she coaxed herself. With all her strength, Rinnie strained and stretched.

Suddenly, the ladder licked her hand.

Rinnie gasped. The world began to rewind. No one was chasing her. The ladder melted from sight. The tree house disappeared, and Rinnie could feel a pillow under her head. She stopped running, and took several quivery breaths. Then she got licked again.

Her hand felt a soft, raggedy lump of fur next to her bed. "Oh, Rascal!" she sighed, then peeped open her eyes. The dog stood waiting patiently for her to wake up. And thank heavens she had—what a nightmare! Her heart was still pounding. Rinnie wondered if she'd ever forget what had happened, or be free from dreams like this.

She leaned over the edge of her bed and rubbed Rascal's ears. "You were a part of that crazy adventure too, weren't ya, boy? Do you have nightmares? I know you miss Mr. Moore. I wish he could've stayed in his house by the lake. But guess what?" she bent down close to whisper, "One of these days we're gonna sneak you into the seniors' home to see him!"

Rascal licked her right on the mouth. "Oh, ick!" Rinnie giggle-groaned and ran for the bathroom. Rascal whimpered when she shut the door between them, but she didn't need the visual of him drinking out of the toilet while she was busy washing off the pooch smooch. He quit scratching on the door soon and ran to join Miss Tizzy, the cat, who was meowing for scraps in the kitchen.

Rinnie brushed her teeth with extra toothpaste, and then got the hair brush from her drawer in the cabinet. As she looked in the mirror, she couldn't help thinking of the dream again. Her heart was still beating a little fast. It was hard to push what had happened last June from her mind. There were too many reminders of how close she'd come to disaster. She was ready for a change of scenery.

In three days she'd be headed to camp—finally. Rinnie contemplated the variety of fun things she'd be doing there: swimming, boating, hiking, and eating s'mores. Her best friend, Erica, would be back from vacation and Rinnie couldn't wait to see her.

"We've got a lot to talk about!" Rinnie told her reflection. A list of subjects crossed her mind—the Raven Cove incident, Miss Tizzy and the kittens, and of course, the new kid in the neighborhood—Nicolas Nedders. Rinnie paused. Maybe she wouldn't mention Nick. She was mad at him now anyway.

He used to be *her* friend, and it'd been cool to have a friend who was a guy, for a change. He had a personality, some intelligence, and an appropriate sense of humor. But ever since her older brother, Squid, and his friends had returned from scout camp, Nick had been hanging out with them, and less with Rinnie—a lot less. He'd made himself at home with the group, and before long was just another monkey in the tree house out back. It was annoying. It wasn't like she was in love with him or anything like that. Heck no—yuck! She just missed talking to him. Oh well—his loss! She was going to camp soon and had more important things to think about.

A troubling recollection wriggled its way into her thoughts. It was the one thing that could spoil camp, if she let it. "I wish I'd never heard that ghost story," Rinnie whispered confidentially to the mirror.

True, she was thirteen, but supernatural, creepy things made her feel like a three-year-old. She pretended to be interested sometimes, so other kids wouldn't think she was weird, but mostly she avoided the subject. Deep down she knew the haunted-camp story was ridiculous, so why did it bother her?

One reason was that she'd experienced a strange feeling the first time she'd gone to that campsite. It wasn't a scary feeling. It was a lonely, searching feeling. She'd figured she was just homesick, until she heard the story from older girls at camp. It still gave her goose bumps.

That's enough! Rinnie shook her head to clear it. The yummy smell of pancakes and bacon snapped her back into reality. She had more pleasant things to think about. There was a lot to do—planning, shopping, and packing. But first there was breakfast.

"Rinnie, are you gonna come and eat? Or should I feed it to the animals?" her mother called from the kitchen. "We need to get going if you want to shop today."

"I'm coming!" Rinnie called back. Hurriedly she put away both brushes and scampered down the hall.

Chapter 2
Mom-Time

Rinnie knew right where she was headed when she and her mom entered the store. Her list was specific. It had to be. She had only so much babysitting money to spend for the things she needed. Mom had given her a few dollars extra to buy a hat, sunscreen, and mosquito repellent, but it was Rinnie's goal to handle the rest on her own.

First on her list was a travel-size tube of toothpaste, unscented deodorant—because perfumy scents attracted critters, particularly bees—and a package of covered elastic bands for her hair. Thank heavens, her haircut mistake had grown out enough that she could put in little braids or stubby pigtails and cover it up with a hat or a big handkerchief. Camp hair was dirty hair by the second day, and the more you kept it out of your face the better.

Next, Rinnie glanced through a close-out rack in the clothing department. She found two bright-colored T-shirts that had been marked down to $4.00 each. She was ecstatic. A camp wardrobe was not about fashion. Sturdy, breathable clothes were all she'd need, nothing fancy, and she had plenty of nothing fancy at home. Still, sometimes it was nice to have something new. But could she afford it? She had to get her secret-sister gifts picked out first.

Each year the girls drew names to see who would be their secret sister for the week. They'd go out of their way to do something special for that girl from Tuesday through Friday. As much as possible it was done anonymously, and often the junior leaders—girls 16 to 18 years old—helped sneak the surprises into the cabin and under the pillow of the recipient. The gifts were gestures of kindness, and not meant to be a financial burden. It was a neat thing to do, and everyone was a little friendlier. You couldn't be too grouchy to others when one of them might be your secret sister.

"It's the thought that counts," the leaders had said. "Be creative, not extravagant."

With this in mind, Rinnie got a six-inch bottle of Super Bubbles from the toy department. She was going to write something like, "May your troubles be like bubbles and float away." It sounded corny. But at camp, corny was cool—especially when it came to secret-sister stuff. It was just a way of saying, "Have a nice day!" So bubbles would work.

Candy worked too, but you weren't supposed to take it—or at least, not much of it. The leaders knew everyone did, but discouraged sugary smells because other critters were attracted to them—sometimes *big* critters! Since she didn't want her secret sister to get eaten by bugs or bears, Rinnie picked only one eat-treat—a candy bar. What she was going to say with it she had no clue, but she'd think of something. While she was at it, Rinnie got a pack of gum for herself, and another candy bar, in case she needed an energy boost on the hike. That is, if it lasted that long.

Her mom suggested an inexpensive flashlight with "Let your light shine" written on it. Alaska summers have so many hours of daylight that you hardly ever needed a flashlight. It'd work fine as a gift though. Okay, she needed only two more things.

They came across a small, ceramic statue of two hugging angels that was engraved: *Friends Stick Together*.

"This would be perfect," her mom said.

"I know. They're darling! But buying that eliminates one of the T-shirts."

"Hmm, hard choice. We need to get going, so decide and we'll check out in five minutes. I'm going to the fabric section."

Rinnie grinned. "In all my life, you've never spent only five minutes in the fabric section."

"Today I will, and beat you to the checkstand."

"I think not!" Rinnie scoffed. She was about to make a challenge, saying, "If I win, you do my laundry for a week," but her mom unexpectedly said, "Go!"

Rinnie was surprised how fast her mom took off. It made her smile. It was great to shop together. Sure they spent time together on cooking and chores, but it was the times like this, doing fun stuff, that was the best of Mom-time.

———

Falling into line behind her mother, Rinnie pretended to be upset, "You cheated!"

"I did not! I told you I was going to the fabric section, and I did."

"Yes, but you didn't get any fabric."

"But I did go there." Her mom held up a spool of black thread.

Rinnie pretended to be annoyed. She loved it when her mother kidded around. Generally, she was a very stressed-out lady. Besides her mom-job, Ruth Cumberland had tons of organizing to do for the Ladies Relief Society. She was always busy cooking this or that, or driving here and there to do things for people, and the phone calls were constant. What could Rinnie do that might give her a mental health break?

With two people still ahead of them, Rinnie got an idea. "Mom, let's read cards. We can use a laugh."

"We really should get going," her mom said, then shrugged. "Oh, why not? It's been a while. But just for a minute."

———

The greeting card aisle was the friendliest place in the store. People talked to each other there. They passed cards back and forth. Rinnie and her mom had a good time. It was amazing how oddball humor could sometimes brighten your day.

Before long, her mom began searching meticulously through some very lovely *Thinking of You* cards. She'd read them carefully, and then glance at the price on the back.

"What are you looking for?" Rinnie asked, after she'd rejected several.

"I can't explain, but I'll know it when I see it," was all her mom would say. Finally, she settled on one with beautiful flowers and gold trim. It was the largest card there. It was also the most expensive. Rinnie was surprised that her mother splurged and bought it.

Rinnie placed her own purchases into two different store bags—one for secret-sister stuff, one for personal stuff. Then it was time to go.

Chapter 3

Boys Will Be Boys

After dinner, Rinnie looked over the gifts she'd bought. She was happy with her choices and just for fun, opened the Super Bubbles and blew through the bubble wand one time. A delicate shower of rainbow spheres danced in the air, and disappeared. "Yup, that'll work," Rinnie said, pleased.

As she started to tighten the lid, her mom called out, "Somebody get the doorbell, please. I'm up to my elbows in bread dough."

"I've got it," Rinnie answered, and set the bubbles down.

Nick was standing on the front porch.

"Hi!" Rinnie said, enthusiastically, forgetting for a second that she was mad at him.

"Hi, Rinnie. I was supposed to come over and play basketball with the guys later, and uh, it's later." Nick smiled.

"Squid's mowing the back lawn. He'll be done soon. Come on in and wait."

"Squid! I still can't believe you call him that," Nick said, as he walked toward the couch. "He gets mad if the guys don't call him J.R. Where does he get *that* from?"

Sitting down across from him in an old recliner, Rinnie explained. "J.R. is for the junior part of Bill Jr. He's named after my dad. He got suspended in third grade for beating up a sixth-grader who teased him about the Squid nickname. We're supposed to call him J.R. outside of home, but he'll always be Squid to me. You could call him that, too."

Nick scoffed. "No thanks, I value my life!"

Miss Tizzy walked by. She hissed and ran off when Nick tried to pet her.

"I don't think your cat likes me."

"That's because you guys keep moving her and the kittens out of the tree house. She thinks it's her territory, and it takes her all day to drag 'em back up there," Rinnie chuckled.

"She's determined, that's for sure."

"Yup." An uncomfortable silence fell between them. Rinnie got up to leave. "See ya later."

Nick blurted out, "Guess what? My mom's moving to Alaska this fall!"

"That's cool!" Rinnie was sincerely glad for him.

"She's afraid there won't be anywhere to shop, or anything to do."

"There are lots of places to shop here—regular stores, souvenir stores, specialty shops, and tons of other places to spend money. And as far as things to do, we also have a symphony here, an opera guild, theatre groups, tons of museums, and plenty of other cultural stuff. You guys should also put in for the Denali Park lottery—you know, where Mount McKinley is?"

"What do you get if you win—a caribou?"

"No, silly! You win the chance to spend a whole day driving through the park in your own car. Usually you have to go by tour bus. We were selected last year. The mountains in the Alaska Range are amazing! It's like looking back through time into the Ice Age. You almost expect to see a mammoth or a saber-tooth tiger walking along. I'll have to show you the pictures sometime. It'll blow you away. We saw a bear with cubs crossing a river, Dall sheep with those big curled horns, and two caribou bulls clashing in battle too."

"Sounds cool."

"What's cool?" Squid interrupted.

"Our Denali Park trip."

"Yeah, but it was hard being cooped up in a car with my family on winding, dirt roads all day."

Rinnie scowled. "It was hard for us too. We had to open the windows a lot because of Mr. I-ate-two-cans-of chili-the-night-before."

Squid nodded proudly. "Yup. It was like a percussion recital."

Nick snickered. Rinnie walked off.

"Enough chitchat. Let's get to the hoops, boy." Squid popped Nick on the shoulder with his fist, and they left.

"You forgot to shut the door," Rinnie called after them.

"Deal with it," Squid called back.

She did—by slamming it. Dang that Squid—talk about annoying! And to think, a lot of the girls she knew thought he was cute. Gross!

Rinnie refocused on her packing. Once all her basic items had been carefully laid out and organized on her bed, she realized how ironic it was that she was now going to roll it all up and cram it into a large duffle bag. She went over the checklist: personal needs, shirts, pants, socks, underwear, pajamas, swimsuit, a hand towel, an extra bath towel, sneakers, hiking boots, a sweater, a hooded sweatshirt, and a coat. It was a lot to take for six days. But in Alaska, you dressed in layers, especially when camping. It could go from warm to chilly rather quickly—sometimes within a few minutes—so it was better to be prepared. On top of this she added her journal, her camp manual, her book of scriptures, and a camera.

Expensive cameras were strongly discouraged because things did get lost at times, and accidents happened. That wasn't a problem for Rinnie. The Cumberlands didn't own an expensive camera. Mom had gotten a digital one for Christmas and told Rinnie that she could take the old camera to camp. There was even a fresh roll of film, so that saved her a little cash.

She almost forgot to roll a pillow and a thin blanket inside her sleeping bag. Thank heavens for the list! Tomorrow night they'd drop off her bedding and clothes at the church to be packed in one big trailer with everyone else's gear, and she'd draw a name for her secret-sister assignment. Then it was only a matter of showing up on Monday morning ready to go.

The plastic crackled as Rinnie scooped all the secret-sister stuff into the store bag. She added two pieces of dark blue construction paper and her favorite silver pen so she could make little cards and write messages. All this she put into the large inside pocket of the backpack she'd carry, leaving space in the smaller outside pocket for last-minute items such as the toothbrush and hairbrush she'd need to use before she left. She also put her personal gum and candy bar in that pocket. There'd be a lot of traveling before they'd get any lunch.

Rinnie smiled into her bedroom mirror. She was almost ready. There was one more decision to make. Reaching under her collar, Rinnie lifted up the delicate gold chain of her favorite necklace. It had three connected hearts, with a tiny rhinestone chip on the center one. To take, or not to take, that was the question. She'd worn it nearly every day since her eleventh birthday. It was a treasured gift from a loving aunt. At camp, jewelry was discouraged. Still, she'd feel practically naked without it, so Rinnie decided it should go.

Chapter 4

Sleepless in Alaska

Sunday had started out as a relaxing day. They'd had an excellent family dinner after church, and in the afternoon they played one-base softball in the backyard while Mom had a nap. Dad and Russell were on one team, Rinnie and Squid on the other. It was enjoyable until Squid got mad at Rinnie for making them lose because she "threw like a girl." Well, duh!

Soon afterwards, Rinnie's dad drove her back to the church so her sleeping bag and belongings could be packed in the big camp trailer. That's when the real trouble began.

First came the bad news. Rinnie had hoped to see her best friend when she dropped her camp stuff off. Instead, she was told that Erica wasn't going to be back in time to go. Rinnie felt totally let down, and could barely think about it without crying.

As if that wasn't enough, when she tried to go to sleep, she was plagued by a nagging feeling that something was wrong, but what? Was it the Camp Kachemak ghost story creeping her out? Possibly. Was it enough to keep her from going? No, but it did worry her. She rubbed her arms to get rid of the goose bumps.

Something else was bothering her. Rinnie tried to sleep, but couldn't get comfortable. She tried reading. That didn't work. Listening to calm music didn't help either. Around midnight, Rinnie gave up trying, and shuffled down the hallway to the kitchen. Her mother was already out there. Poor Mom. Sometimes the only quiet moment she had to relax all day was late at night, sitting at the kitchen table, writing to people. She did that a lot.

"Who are the notes for this time?" Rinnie asked, pulling up a chair.

"In this pile are thank-you cards for the people who helped with the luncheon after the funeral last week. And in this pile are sympathy cards for the family of the person who died."

"Oh." Rinnie noticed that the specially selected greeting card her mom had bought was on the table. Whoever was getting that one was sure lucky!

Ruth Cumberland set her pen down. "Now, changing the subject, what are you doing up?"

"Can't sleep."

"Too excited?"

"A little, but mostly bummed out about Erica. I should've figured it out when she didn't call me this week to say she was home."

"I'm sure she'd rather be home than sitting around in California with a broken ankle."

"I know," Rinnie said, scrunching up her face. "I wish she'd never gone to Disneyland!"

"I'll bet she does too at this point. It wasn't a thrilling day for her, falling down a bunch of steps while she was taking a picture. Poor thing! You can't blame her for staying with cousins instead of riding twenty-four hundred miles back to Alaska in a cramped car."

"Yeah, but we put on our registration form that we wanted to be in the same cabin," Rinnie whined. "It just would've been more fun."

"Oh, you'll have a good time. What about the secret-sister thing? Whose name did you draw?"

"Some girl I don't even know—Jessica Jeffries."

"Jessica Jeffries? Hmm … oh, I know who that is. She just moved here. Hey, there's a new adventure for you. She has quite a story!"

"I'm too tired for a new adventure. It's easier to be grumpy."

"And you'll be extra grumpy if you don't get some sleep, kiddo. How about I make us some hot chocolate and toast, and then you can go back to bed? In the meantime, you can write the last five thank-yous for me."

"You'd better write 'em. I'll cook."

As she spread butter and grape jelly, Rinnie's mind began to wander. "Mom, do you believe in ghosts?" she half-mumbled.

Her mom looked up. "What'd you say?"

"Nothing. Here's your toast."

———•——

Twenty minutes later, as Rinnie was dozing off in her warm, snuggly bed, she wondered what had caused the bothersome feeling earlier. But her curiosity soon gave way to relaxation, as she listened to her mom humming hymns out at the table.

Chapter 5

The Big Day

Monday morning was bright and sunny. By 6 a.m. it was already starting to get warm. Normally, Rinnie would've been as excited as the rest of the girls, but she felt awful. Her stomach was wishing she'd eaten more of the scrambled eggs her dad had fixed. He'd also tried to make her smile by telling amusing tales of tourists who rode his bus. Unfortunately, Rinnie's funny bone wasn't awake yet.

A tired haze enveloped her body. If Mom had been waiting with her like last year, Rinnie could've crawled into the back seat of the car and snoozed until it was time to go. But Mom had slept in and Dad had only stopped for a minute to talk to the leaders, then gone to work. After he left, she found a patch of lawn in the shade and lay down using her backpack as a pillow.

The sweet scent of flowers and pine trees mixed with a fresh-earth fragrance as the last of the morning dew melted away. Rinnie loved that smell and breathed in deeply, closing her eyes. Camp was going to be like this—and then some. At least that was something to look forward to!

The rest of the girls were chattering like chickens. The general jabber was punctuated periodically by one loud voice, asking, "Do you like my new shoes?" over and over. It was Carla Clupps' irritating voice, connected to Carla Clupps' irritating self. She wasn't one of Rinnie's favorite people.

Rinnie had tried to befriend her when the Clupp family first moved into the area, but it had never really clicked between them. Carla had a very high opinion of herself.

She also had a one-track mind. Her favorite topic of conversation was boys, boys, boys, boys, boys—especially one boy, Rinnie's brother, Squid, or J.R., rather. Carla loved to probe for information about him, and never took the hint that he wasn't the least bit interested in her. Luckily, Carla's new shoes were keeping her occupied that morning, which was fine with Rinnie.

The later it got, the louder the group became. Chicks sounding like chickens. Rinnie chuckled at her own lame joke. She needed a nap! Hopefully she could sleep as they drove to Camp Kachemak. Why weren't they leaving? It was past six-thirty—the time they'd all agreed to be there. But the leaders didn't seem to be in a hurry. They were waiting for one more somebody to arrive.

Things were always late getting started. It was practically a church tradition, so Rinnie shouldn't have been surprised. She might've even complained out loud about it, except that a couple of the times in the past when they'd waited, she'd been the one who'd arrived late and had been glad not to be left behind.

Rinnie felt someone walk near her. She squinted to see who it was. "Hi Carla," she said flatly, and closed her eyes again.

"Are you alright?"

"Yup." Rinnie tried to be cordial. After all, what if she was Carla's secret sister? But her patience wasn't awake yet either, so as soon as Carla started her usual ramble, Rinnie closed her eyes even tighter and tried to think happy thoughts.

"Do you like my new shoes?"

"Yeah, they're great."

"You didn't even look!"

"Yes, I did. They're new, right?"

"Yeah, but I already told you that. So, if you looked, what color are they?"

"A lovely color, uh …" Rinnie stalled, and took a quick peek. "Very pink!"

"Thank you. How's J.R. doing? He's so handsome! I saw him yesterday, but he didn't say anything. Must've been preoccupied. I wore my blue dress. That's his favorite color, right? I'll bet he noticed. Do you think he noticed? I tried to get light blue sneakers in case he came today. But they didn't come in my size. I have narrow feet. Most people have wide feet. Anyway, the pink ones are very festive, don't you think?"

"Yes, festive—very." Rinnie tried not to grind her molars as she listened. No one could talk faster than Carla Clupp once she got on a roll.

"Does J.R. ever ask about me? Did he say to tell me hi? Do you think I should call him? Does he have his own phone number? I do. I could email him. Do you know his address? He keeps forgetting to give it to me. I gave him a school picture last fall. It's hanging up in his room, right?"

Rinnie wanted to yell, "Take a breath!" Listening to it all made her dizzy, and she faced a big dilemma. Should she tell the poor girl that Squid had purposely not given her his email address, and had put her picture on his dart board? Naw, she'd never believe it.

"It'd be cool if we got in the same cabin. You could tell me about other things J.R. likes, and just wait till you hear the fantastic ghost stories I have to tell."

Carla Clupp *and* ghost stories? Rinnie shuddered.

Carla didn't notice. She continued, "I belong to this Internet group that knows all about supernatural stuff, so watch out!" Carla smiled, proudly, then switched back to her favorite subject. "I was *really* hoping J.R. would be dropping you off this morning."

"Is that why you wore so much makeup?" Rinnie's eyes popped open. She hadn't meant to say that out loud. She winced, worried about Carla's reaction. It didn't seem to faze her, and certainly didn't end the conversation.

"I always wear makeup. It keeps my skin soft and moistur-ized. Besides, my mom sells Avon and I get a discount, so I can wear it all I want to. You ought to try some. It might help." Carla said, smiling like a satisfied Siamese cat.

Rinnie's eyes opened wider. Might help what? What was

Carla insinuating? Ooh! The blood rushed into Rinnie's cheeks. She almost said something she might've been sorry for, but instead closed her eyes again. "Remember the rules flyer they had us staple in our manuals? Camp is a makeup-free zone."

"Well, we aren't there yet, are we?" Carla said, and turned on her heel and walked away.

Less than five seconds later, Rinnie heard Carla ask someone else if they liked her new shoes. Pink sneakers? Who in her right mind brings pink sneakers to camp? Rinnie sighed. Please don't make me be in the same cabin with her! Please, oh please, oh please!

Chapter 6

Camp Kachemak, Here We Come!

Five leaders were going to camp. They took turns teaching classes, supervising activities, and keeping things organized. Five young women were assigned to each cabin, and one of the leaders stayed in the cabin at night. That leader was the person the girls were to go to first if there was a problem.

For camp, the leaders picked nicknames. It was easier to remember than Mrs. This or Sister That. This year Ashley Anderson's mom and Tracey Wilson's grandma were in charge of crafts, and would also help the girls pass skills such as knot tying and fire building. Their nicknames were Snip and Snap. Jan Beckham's mom had been in the military, so putting her in charge of classes such as outdoor survival, canoeing, and hiking was a perfect fit, just like her nickname—Sarge. Paula Jensen's mom was the main leader. She said that she'd picked Echo for her camp name, because she usually had to repeat things several times before the girls paid attention. She had the final say on all decisions and made sure that there was an uplifting message every day.

Six junior leaders, or Juls as they were called—were older girls who'd been there and done that camp-wise, so they spent the week helping as needed, and keeping everyone enthusiastic. Their nickname sounded like *jewels*, and it fit. The younger girls admired them, and they were nice to everyone. Of course, they were extra nice to Rinnie at times because of her good-looking brother. But at least they weren't annoying about it.

And then there was Cookie.

Cookie's real name was Roberta Cookson, but she'd been the camp chef for so many years that people called her Cookie all year long. By the way she put together a meal you knew that you'd been fed, and she made it look easy. She was the roundest of all the leaders there, but not one of them would've challenged her to a foot race.

Cookie Cookson was a smart, mostly easygoing lady. She knew a lot about a lot of things and was interesting to talk to. But she could be blunt. It was said that "if Cookie grumbles, camp crumbles," and few things upset her more than gawkers. If you came around while she was preparing food, you'd better not sit there.

Two dads were at camp at all times. To keep things simple, the girls referred to them as Dad 1 and Dad 2. They drove a big truck with a camper, and pulled the long trailer packed with all the gear and the girls' stuff. Their truck was parked near the entrance to Camp Kachemak, and they served as bouncers for unwanted guests—be it bears or boys. They also helped teach skills such as wood chopping and axe sharpening, and they patrolled the area often, each carrying a pistol. Rinnie had never seen the pistols taken out of their holsters. There was usually no need, but this was Alaska, so better safe than sorry. The camp dads had left before Rinnie arrived. With the load they were pulling, they needed to get a head start.

A little after seven, Echo asked the girls to gather around. "We'll make cabin and travel assignments, then we'll be ready to go."

Rinnie glanced through the crowd. She recognized everyone there. Where was this new person who was supposed to be her secret sister?

"We know that a lot of you picked specific friends you wanted to bunk with, but we've decided that this year we're going to do it differently."

A disappointed groan rippled through the group.

"Oh, come on. It'll be fun! You'll be traveling with the same girls that you're cabin mates with. This'll give you a chance to get some camaraderie going, work on your cabin decor plans, and formulate ideas for the skit you'll present later this week. Listen for your name and leader information. As soon as we're finished with assignments, you can go to your leader's vehicle. The first group is …" Echo paused when a car drove up.

Everyone turned to see who they'd been waiting for. Rinnie hardly recognized Amber Call when she stepped out of the car. She knew this girl, had been friends with her all through school. They'd sort of drifted apart in the last eight months, but Rinnie still cared. What in the world had happened to her? Her beautiful auburn hair was black; blacker than the blackest black Rinnie had ever seen. Her face was pale, and her eyes smudged, as if she'd recently taken off a lot of makeup in a hurry. Obviously annoyed, she rolled her eyes in response to every comment made by her father.

"Oh good, we're all here now," Echo said, and began calling out names.

To Rinnie it sounded suspiciously like gym class—the girls whose last names started with A were assigned to Cabin A. The leftover A-name girls went into Cabin B with the B-name girls.

"Cabin C girls, your leader is Cookie. That should be easy to remember."

Rinnie knew that there were enough C-name girls to fill a whole cabin, so she wasn't surprised to hear the names Amber Call, Carla Clupp, Lynnette Cole, Kiana Crowley, and Lorinda Cumberland called out. Rinnie shook her head. It figures!

Carla ran up beside her. "I know. I'm upset too. We've got to stick together and not let that weirdo ruin it for us!" she whispered conspiratorially, and ran off to warn the others in their group.

Not let the *weirdo* ruin it for us? As Rinnie trudged toward the van, she whimpered, "It's gonna to be a *long* week!"

Rinnie elected to sit as far back in the vehicle as she could. Maybe if she fell asleep she'd wake up and discover that this morning had all been a bad dream and she could begin again. Frustrated, she took a bite out of her candy bar, then shoved her backpack under the left side of her head and leaned against the window.

Out in the parking lot, she heard an adult's coaxing voice, "Come on, honey. You need to go now."

Rinnie turned to see who was talking.

"*Please* get out. They're waiting. You'll be okay, I promise."

A thin, dark-haired girl slowly got out of the car. She looked scared to death.

"*Hello*, Jessica," Rinnie whispered.

A few minutes later, the girls' camp caravan finally hit the road.

Chapter 7

Rackety Ride

There was a lot going on in that van, and plenty of noise. Rinnie closed her eyes and listened.

Cookie had wisely selected Amber to be copilot on the drive, and she was busy loading the CD player and taking other directions. As the ride continued, Cookie began to ask genuinely interested questions. What had Amber been doing all summer? What kinds of music did she enjoy? Was she looking forward to school starting in a few weeks?

The school thing got Cookie started on a comical story about her junior high days, and before long they were both laughing. Amber's harsh attitude softened and she sounded more like the old friend Rinnie had known for years.

Eventually Cookie asked her about the decision to have her ears pierced four times, and since the rules stated only one pair of simple earrings were allowed per girl, how did she choose which to leave home?

"The ones I've had for a while can go without anything in them for a few days. The one I got done last week needs to have posts in all the time until it heals. I might get a nose gem for my birthday."

That started another conversation.

In the meantime, in the middle seat, after Carla had exhausted the topic of her shoes—how much they'd cost and how fabulous they were—brainstorming began about cabin décor. Lynnette efficiently wrote things down in a notebook.

There were twenty cabins at the campsite. They weren't much more than shanties made with ancient, rough-hewn logs and rusty metal roofs that had been smeared with tar. The attached porches seemed like they'd detach if someone jumped up and down too hard. The front corners of these had been propped up with big rocks just in case.

No one knew when the cabins were built. They'd outlived anyone who could remember. It was a mystery how they'd withstood so many Alaska winter storms. But each year the first group to use them slathered on a thick new layer of whitewash. It might have been what kept them together. Each group after that was allowed to repaint the door with a design that the girls chose to signify who was staying there. By summer's end the paint was caked on and cracking. Still it was neat to see how each one got personalized.

Brainstorming to Carla meant that she talked and others listened, so every time Lynnette started to say, "We could like …" or, "What about …" Carla talked even faster.

Kiana, who sat by Rinnie, leaned forward to get in on the conversation, listening intently, nervously biting the side of her finger and nodding a lot. Kiana was Erica's cousin. She was a bit on the chubby side, sweet, very shy, and didn't often speak up. That biting-her-finger thing Rinnie didn't understand, but whatever.

Lynnette and Rinnie had been on the same team for Battle of the Books in elementary school. She'd changed a lot since then. Her hair got blonder every month and she'd started saying *like* a lot. Everybody said *like* a lot, but Lynnette said it ten times more. She'd gone into a popular group at school, and like all of them like talked like that.

It was obvious that Carla had glommed onto Lynnette to be her bunkmate and new best friend of the week. But as smart and outspoken as Lynnette was, Rinnie wondered how long that would last. Oh well, if it kept her from answering endless questions about her brother, Squid, it was worth it!

———

After they'd been driving about an hour, Cookie asked, "How's it going back there? Made any big decisions yet?"

"Not yet," Carla said, "I was thinking that we could wait and see the cabin when we get there—see what we have to work with. I'm sure some inspiration will pop right out at us."

"Hmm. Does that work for the rest of you?"

Lynnette spoke up. "I was like thinking we could do like 'C's the day!' You know—the letter C, since we're Cabin C and like all our last names start with a C."

Carla snickered, and then pretended to cough.

"Oh, I get it," Kiana said, excitedly. "It has a double meaning. It's like 'Seize the day,' and that's actually an inspirational saying, so it could work."

"Sounds great to me," Cookie said.

"But—but we don't have to choose now. We should wait," Carla protested.

"Why? It's one less decision you'll have to make when you get there. You can get on to doing other things."

Carla was insistent. "But it's an important decision, we don't need to rush."

"It's a door, for crying out loud, not fine art. Sure, you want it to look good but you don't need to get carried away." Cookie went full steam ahead. "How many of you vote for Lynnette's 'C's the day?'"

Lynnette raised her hand. Kiana raised hers.

"See? That's not a majority," Carla gloated.

Amber grinned as she turned around to raise her hand. Rinnie opened one eye and raised her hand about the same time.

To no one's surprise, Carla pouted the rest of the way. Lynnette, Amber, and Kiana decided on the door design and what colors to use. Rinnie finished her nap.

Maybe the leaders had been inspired to put Carla in that cabin after all. Cookie knew how to handle her. She'd had lots of practice. They were related.

Chapter 8

Organized Chaos

As they pulled into camp, Cookie said, "Here's your first set of instructions. Before you unpack, take the broom from the corner and give the cabin a good sweep. Check under the bunks for spider webs or voles."

"Ooh! Gross!" was the general response.

Cookie continued, "After that, head on down to the pavilion for a snack. There's also a craft class that everyone needs to attend, and then you'll have some free time."

———

Camp Kachemak looked like an Alaska postcard with its rustic old cabins, framed with wildflowers, birch, and pine trees, nestled near a teal blue lake. A spectacular backdrop of distant mountains, crowned with a touch of snow on the highest peaks, completed the picture-perfect view.

However, the cabins weren't the first place the girls ran to once the van had stopped. The brakes had barely been applied, when the doors flew open and the girls piled out in rapid succession and ran for the porta-potties.

Since Rinnie was the last one out of the van, she saw that Cookie had taken Carla aside. What Rinnie overheard was, "I mean it, Carla, I want you to let it go, and be nice."

Carla stomped her foot and said, "Aunt Cookie, I'm always nice!"

"This week, you should be a little *nicer*."

Rinnie didn't stay to hear more. The lineup was getting longer by the second, so she ran for it.

Three types of bathroom facilities were available at Camp Kachemak. The first option, of course, was the bushes. But with a camp full of girls, this wasn't really an option. It was generally discouraged for several reasons: Pine cones made lousy toilet paper, there wasn't much privacy, you could interrupt a bear using the bushes, or you could be interrupted by a bear as *you* were using the bushes. At the very least, you ran the risk of getting a mosquito bite in a place that was embarrassing to scratch.

The second type, and the one closest to the cabins, was an outhouse. There was one of these for every three cabins. Each came complete with cobwebs, wooden seats that pinched when you sat down, and usually no toilet paper. If there was any, it hung on a nail and was so dingy that you had to unroll about a yard of it before you could see that it had ever been white. There was never a waiting line for these small, sturdy fortresses, which, like the cabins, had been there many moons. They looked like they belonged in a hillbilly cartoon, except there was no crescent-shaped cutout on the door. In fact, there was very little ventilation except for a circle of heavy-wire mesh just below the roofline on two sides—another reason that these were the least favorite choice. Your use of these depended on how desperate you were and how long you could hold your breath.

The most commonly used facilities were the blue portable toilets that were rented each summer. These were modern except that they didn't flush, and usually had toilet paper. A truck came to empty them twice a week. The main problem with them was that the door didn't always close tight, and they rocked if there was a strong breeze or an earth tremor. The smell inside wasn't exactly roses, but a can of bathroom spray was supplied. The porta-potties were across the field from the cabins, not too far from the pavilion and halfway to the lake.

Rinnie wasn't the only one who ran across the field. There was a stampede in that direction from all the vehicles. It would be one of the few times when this happened. For the most part, everyone avoided the potties as long as possible.

As she waited her turn, Rinnie saw her secret sister, Jessica, standing farther down the line. People were chatting excitedly around her, yet she stood head down, not speaking to anyone, and making no eye contact.

What was with this girl? Rinnie's mom always said, "Everyone has a story," but how did you get to know someone who wouldn't talk to you, or even look at you?

The twenty old cabins were numbered. Cabin one was set up for first aid. Cabin two, which held miscellaneous supplies and a small refrigerator, was the site of the leaders' planning meetings during free time. Cabin number three was lacking a door, so the cabin C girls ended up in cabin six. However, since they'd been grouped alphabetically, they referred to the cabins that way too. Rinnie and crew left their gear on the porch and went inside to inspect.

Inside, the log cabins were plainer than ever. There were three sets of bunk beds. Some of them had cotton wadding mattresses, some didn't. As stained and dusty as the mattresses were, if you didn't get one, you didn't feel bad. The girls were each supposed to bring an air or foam mattress, just in case. Very old curtains covered the thinnest window glass Rinnie had ever seen, and there were hundreds of names of previous campers etched into the interior logs. A large bare bulb in the center of the ceiling proved that the cabin had electricity, though you didn't leave your hand on the light switch more than a second, unless you wanted a shock. Luckily, it was late-July in Alaska so they'd still have natural light at night.

"Home sweet home, girls," Amber announced. "Somebody open the window. Let's air this place out. I volunteer to sweep. I'll even check for spider webs. I'm not afraid."

"Wait a minute. You can't volunteer. We all have to decide on the chores," Carla insisted.

"Chores?"

"Yes. Every day someone has to come back after breakfast to sweep and take out the garbage. We have to decide who does it on what day."

"Or we could go alphabetically." Kiana suggested.

"Works for me," Rinnie said.

Lynnette shrugged.

"So, I guess that's a majority. Hmm, who would be first, alphabetically? Oh, I guess it's me!" Amber said, and got the broom from the corner. "Wouldn't want you to get those new shoes dirty."

She and Carla exchanged fake smiles.

As they waited outside, Carla pulled Lynnette aside and walked off a few feet. Not surprisingly, her voice could still be heard. "I want you to share a bunk with me. I don't have anything in common with those other girls."

"Okay, but like I get first choice of top or bottom."

"Fine," Carla agreed. "Now, there's one other thing …"

"What's that?"

"You gotta quit voting against me."

Lynnette appeared apprehensive when she rejoined the others on the porch.

A few minutes later Amber proclaimed, with a bow, "All done, ladies. Carpe bunkum—enter and seize a bunk."

After making a stop at the cooking pavilion, they headed over to see what the mandatory craft project was. It was a mailbox. Each girl was given a shiny, one-gallon storage can with an opaque plastic lid to write her name on and decorate. Five of these fit into a square plastic crate to be left out on the porch of each cabin.

"Remember, these cans have to be emptied or the crate taken inside at night or our squirrel friends may steal the lids, or the goodies," Snip warned.

"Or the blasted magpies will start pecking into things!" Snap added.

Rinnie drew a little flower border around the outside edge of her lid. What a handy idea, she thought, as she wrote her name with a dark pink marker and outlined it in black. Not worrying about how to sneak things into other cabins would make secret-sister deliveries less complicated, and the junior leaders could do other things besides be messengers. Rinnie just had to find out which cabin Jessica was in. She was sorry she hadn't paid attention as the names were being called out.

Free time filled in two hours of time after lunch each day. Camp Kachemak reverberated with the sound of voices. Some of the girls took advantage of the unusually warm day to swim in the roped-off area of the lake. Several played water balloon volleyball in a game that the Juls had organized. The leaders had a meeting scheduled in the supply cabin. Rinnie wondered if they were actually hiding out to eat chocolate or take a nap.

She planned to stretch out and relax. She needed to deal with her disappointment, and get over it. Unfortunately, her bad attitude was still in charge, so Rinnie arranged her sleeping bag and crawled on top. She was an upper bunk person.

Being on the upper bunk had advantages and disadvantages. For instance, if you were on the bottom bunk and there was an earthquake, you might get smashed by the person on the top bunk. But as old as the cabins were, if there was an earthquake that big, the roof would squash the top-bunk person before she squashed the person on the bottom bunk. Either way, it wouldn't be pleasant!

Another advantage of being a top-bunk person was that you had a bit more privacy and a nifty shelf along the wall that you could put things on. You had to dust off the carcasses of dead insects first though. You also hoped you wouldn't roll too far while you were asleep, or you'd wake up staring up at the bottom of the shelf and feel like you were in a coffin.

However, Rinnie didn't need to worry about rude awakenings. Sleep was not an option. A pesky mosquito buzzed around her head and no sooner had she squashed that one when two or three others showed up. Birds squawked and chirped in the trees above the cabin. They didn't sound thrilled about having their space invaded by another group. A commotion came from the camp dads too, as they played with the four-wheeler that Echo's husband had let them borrow for the week. To top it all off, Carla was yelling at someone for getting water all over her new pink sneakers.

Trying to drown all this out took extra time and energy, but it helped in one respect. When the camp was crawling with activity, the unsettling sensation Rinnie felt wasn't noticeable. Maybe the ghost avoided crowds. It was fine by her. Ignoring the feeling was high on her to-do list.

———

"Dinnertime, Cinderella. Or should I say, Rindercella?" Kiana giggled.

"I think you've got me mixed up with Sleeping Beauty," Rinnie moaned. "It was a nice try though." She slowly rolled off the bunk, landing squarely on her feet.

"Wow, you're good."

"Thanks," Rinnie said, though she knew what she'd done was nothing exceptional. Kiana was just easily impressed. "So, who was Carla yelling at earlier?"

Kiana's face reddened. "Me. I made this really awesome catch when we were playing water balloon volleyball. I should say I *almost* made it. I had it right in my hands, and then it broke."

"And it got her new shoes wet, right?"

"Wow, you're *really* good!"

"Not really. When Carla's upset you don't have to have ESP. I heard it all the way up here."

"She sent me to get another pair. She thinks I did it on purpose. Called me an idiot."

"She what?" Rinnie spun Kiana around by the shoulders.

"Look under that bunk. See the boots and one pair of shoes on the right side?"

"Yeah."

"Those are Lynnette's. Now see the boots and the three pair of shoes on the left?"

"Carla's?"

"Yup."

"Wow, do you think she brought enough?" Kiana snickered.

"And then some. So, who's the idiot? She brought the new pink monstrosities just to show off. Don't worry about it. They'll dry."

"Okay. Thanks."

Rinnie calmed down. "Now, *please* tell me there's something yummy for dinner!"

"Taco salads, hot rolls, and watermelon."

"Ooh, Cookie's hot rolls are the best. Race ya there!"

Chapter 9

Echoed Greetings

The Juls got the first campfire off to a rousing start by singing songs and trying to memorize the girls' names as they gathered. When everyone was there, Echo began the meeting.

"Welcome, ladies! Hope you're having a good time so far. We're pleased that all arrived safe and sound. I know you were disappointed not to be able to go canoeing today, but the scouts will be dropping them off tomorrow."

There was some applause and a few hoots.

"Don't get too excited—the canoes are staying, the scouts aren't."

A few boos were heard.

"Oh, cut that out," Echo shook her finger. "You know the rules about boys at camp."

There was general laughter.

"Speaking of contact from the outside world ..." Echo held up a cell phone. "We've collected four of these already today. Girls, you know they were on the *Absolutely Do Not Bring to Camp* side of the rules list. There are several reasons that you don't need one here.

"Reason number one: the closest pizza place is a hundred miles away, and they don't deliver this far out. Reason number two: losing a cell phone is expensive, and it makes parents very cranky. Besides that, the reception is lousy here—trust me! Reason number three: your mom, your boyfriend, your cat, your dog, and your goldfish will all survive if they don't hear your lovely voice for a few days. It might even make them miss you more.

"You know the cell phone rule also applies to CD players, iPods, etcetera. If you're feeling anxious or homesick, please talk to your leader, or come to me. We'll help you cope, or help you get through your electronics withdrawal.

"Now, a few more reminders. Candy and junk food are no-no's. We realize that a few treats get brought for secret-sister gifts. These should be small and consumed immediately. Don't go overboard. If we find somebody's got a stash the size of Willy Wonka's chocolate factory, we *will* make other arrangements for it. Also, hiding goodies in your pillowcase will only attract mice or voles faster, so make your choice—mice or munchies?

"Watch your trash in general, please. If you see something, dispose of it properly—even if you weren't the one who dropped it.

"No perfume. No makeup—there's no one here to impress. No shaving of legs, especially not in the pan we use to heat water for oatmeal. There's no tactful way of describing how it ruins breakfast when tiny hairs are found!"

Several gagging sounds came from the group, and a couple of the Juls looked embarrassed.

"No squirt guns. Water balloons are only allowed for certain activities. Sorry if these rules seem rigid, but things evolve that way when there've been problems in the past. If you're unclear about any of them, read your camp manual again, or talk to a leader.

"Now for a couple of must-do's. Everyone must come to the campfire at night. Mosquitoes will bug us, but if we're all here, the odds of getting eaten alive by the blasted buzzers are less. Share the wealth, you know."

Some people chuckled. Most just swatted the nearest mosquito.

"One more must. You *must* come to flag raising every morning at 6:40. The camp dads will sound the wake-up call at six-thirty."

There was massive grumbling.

Echo ignored it. "We don't care if you come to flag raising

in your pj's or wrapped in your sleeping bag. Just get here! You'll have time to finish getting dressed afterwards. Now, the Juls have information about neat free-time activities that have been planned for the week. Then we'll turn the time over to our guest speaker, Ranger Dan of the Park Service."

Chapter 10

The Bear Truth

Ranger Dan was there to give the campers a refresher course on how to get along with the outdoor inhabitants of the state. Having brothers who were scouts, Rinnie had heard all the wild animal what-not-to-do's, but it was fun to watch Ranger Dan work a crowd. A middle-aged man with a graying mustache, he was a virtual fountain of knowledge, and had a sarcastic sense of humor. Rinnie understood the humor. Her dad was like that too.

"Good evening, ladies," he began. "Most of you know what I'm here to talk about. I'll be as brief as possible so you can get on to the most important part of the evening— marshmallow roasting."

A few girls clapped. Someone called out, "Alright!"

Ranger Dan made the "quiet down" gesture with his hands and then continued. "How many of you have noticed some of our clever marmots, cute squirrels, or pretty little birds since you got here?"

Several hands went up.

"Glad to see that we have an observant group. One key element to staying safe in Alaska is—*be observant*. Here are a few other things to remember. *Never* try to hand-feed *any* animals. Even the cute ones bite. They know where to find food and what to eat. They aren't going to starve if you don't share your garlic-flavored onion chips. They might even get alienated from their clan if you do because they don't have breath mints." The ranger paused for a reaction to his humor. There was none, so he went on.

"At the Park Service, we have a saying that goes: A fed animal is a dead animal. If they lose their fear of people, they can become dangerous and have to be put down. Put down is a nice way of saying 'killed.' So let's try not to cause that, okay? The animals may be curious about you, but they don't want to be held, or petted, or taken home. They're not your new best friends, and if you try to see how close you can get, they *will* respond. To them you're one of two things: a threat, or a meal. Animals have sharp beaks, teeth, or claws to help them survive. You'll want to avoid these.

"I noticed that your volleyball net is still up. I suggest that you take it down at night so that moose don't get tangled up in it. All kinds of things can get caught on those big antlers of theirs, so be careful with what you leave hanging around in areas where they forage.

"Speaking of moose, they aren't geeky doofuses like Bullwinkle. They're not tame. A moose calf can weigh up to three hundred pounds by the time it's five months old. There are several mothers with calves in this area. Some even have twins. But trust me, you don't want to know what a thirteen-hundred-pound mama moose will do to you if you try to take a close-up of her offspring. Use your zoom lens, for Pete's sake, unless you want a stompin'!

"Adult moose are often bigger than a horse. Make noise when you're out and about so you don't startle them. Moose have the right-of-way. Give a mother with a calf plenty of room, and *never* block the path of a bull moose when he's looking for a girlfriend. They have one-track minds, and you have to watch where they're going, because they won't. A confrontation would feel like being run over by a sixteen-hundred-pound boulder with hooves."

Rinnie certainly agreed with the last comment. More than once she'd been riding in a car when a bull moose had run right out in front of vehicles. Traffic came to a complete halt until the animal got all the way across the highway, because if a moose and a car collided, it was usually fatal for the animal and the car, and sometimes for the people.

Ranger Dan took a quick swig of water from his canteen. "Now, about the bears … First let me ask, how many of you have seen a story on the Internet about a twelve-foot Alaska grizzly bear who weighed two thousand pounds, tore a cabin apart, ate one person for lunch, and the other person for dessert?"

Carla's hand shot up the fastest.

"Well, that story is an urban legend!"

"No way!" Carla challenged him. "I've seen the picture!"

"Yup, it's a dang scary picture too. The story isn't accurate though, but it works around a campfire if you want kids to go right to bed afterwards. You leaders should remember that.

"Let's talk about bear facts. First of all, male polar bears can average a thousand pounds, but there haven't been any in this area of the state since the Ice Age—and I'm not talking about the movie."

Groans came from many of the listeners.

"Kodiak bears are usually less than a thousand pounds, and the eleven-footers are rather scarce. There have been a few bigger than that, but not a lot. Your average male grizzly bear weighs five to six hundred pounds, and females usually weigh less. Bears don't stand up and walk on their hind feet when they attack, unless they work in Hollywood. I'm telling you this so you can rest at night without worrying about a furry monster ripping the roof off your cabin.

"Yes, bears have killed and eaten people in Alaska, but only sixty in the last hundred years. It's more likely that people who have bear encounters end up injured. However, those injuries can be devastating. It's not good to surprise a bear. When hiking be loud, and stay with your crowd.

"*Never* go off alone in the wilderness. It's not a smart thing to do in general, not just for the sake of bear safety. Some people think they have a unique connection with bears. They claim it would be an honor to become bear poo—which is technically called scat. But becoming bear scat is *horribly* painful, and people usually change their minds in the middle of the process. By then, it's too late.

The best safety tool you have is your *brain*! Avoid conflict and confrontation.

"Stay far away from a mother with cubs. Those babies don't want to be cuddled, and that mama doesn't need a babysitter. When you're hiking around, plan it so you aren't walking blindly into areas that bears frequent. Are there any questions?"

"What about wearing bear bells?" Ashley Anderson asked.

Ranger Dan smiled. "I refer to them sometimes as 'dinner bells,' and sure wouldn't want my safety to depend on a little tinkling sound. Lower-pitched sounds are better, like gruffly yelling, 'Hey, bear!'

"If you're with a bunch of people like this, there's usually plenty of noise. If you're away from the crowd, do things that will take away the element of surprise. Talk to yourself or sing songs."

Lynnette raised her hand. "Is it true that you shouldn't like run away from a bear?"

"Good question. Usually not. They may see you as fleeing prey and go after you. They can run up to thirty miles an hour, so you *can't* outrun a bear, *even uphill*. However—if you're closer to an *unlocked* vehicle or cabin, run. If you're closer to the bear, don't run. If it's a grizzly, you should roll up in a ball, with your arms and hands covering your head and neck, and play dead. They'll usually swat you a couple of times, they may even chomp once or twice, but as soon as they've determined that you're not a threat they'll leave. If it's a black bear do *not* play dead. Get large and loud and fight back with anything you can get your hands on—shovels, rocks, branches. Black bear rarely attack *unless* they consider you prey, and when they do, they're more likely to chomp and keep chomping."

Kiana anxiously asked, "Are there any bears in this area right now?"

"There are black bears and grizzlies scattered throughout the area. Mostly we only see a flash of them as they hurry to get out of our way. But we have had one complaint around here about a certain three-hundred pound black bear. We call him Booger because he leaves a slimy path of destruction wherever he goes. He's not afraid of people, and that makes him hazardous. If you see him, let us know immediately. Otherwise, just follow the guidelines we talked about and you'll be safe among the animals. And *remember*—you're a guest in their house this week. You wouldn't want them coming into *your* house and messing things up, right? Please be respectful, not neglectful. Thank you!"

Everyone clapped.

"Thank you for coming, Ranger Dan."

He grinned. "You're all very welcome. I only have one more thing to say ... Bring on the marshmallows!"

All the girls cheered.

Chapter 11

Rickety Rest

Rinnie was glad that day was over. Normally, spending the night on the hard, rickety bunks would've kept her awake. But she was sure all she had to do was get into her pj's, and she'd be sound asleep.

"We like need to talk about our skit," Lynnette suggested.

"We can do that while we hike. Right now, while Cookie's not here, let's tell ghost stories!" Carla said mischievously.

Lynnette jumped back in. "Okay, but can I like tell you about an idea first?"

"Later!"

Lynnette looked hurt. Amber looked irritated.

"Telling spooky stories at church camp seems kind of wrong," Kiana pointed out.

Carla scowled at her. "Don't be such a baby!"

Rinnie hoped to avoid the topic. "Please lower your volume. I'm going to sleep!" she said, yawning.

"Fine, spoilsport, we'll proceed without you."

Amber mumbled something, and rolled over on her sleeping bag, her back to the group. Like Rinnie, she was an upper-bunk person.

Carla didn't appreciate losing half her audience. Lynnette, an upper-bunker too, seemed resigned to listen to Carla for the sake of peace in the neighborhood. "Are you gonna like tell the one about the couple sitting at lovers' lane and ..."

"No. Everyone knows that one," Carla interrupted. "They were kissing, blah, blah, blah. She had a bad feeling, blah, blah, blah. She made him take her home. He drove off like a wild man and when he opened her door to let her out, there was a bloody hand hook hanging on the door handle. Big deal!"

"Oh, sick!" Kiana shuddered.

"You haven't heard that one?"

"No."

"Brother! It's as old as my grandma and totally unbelievable. I want to tell you a real, scary story. It's about Lost Girl Lake—which used to be the name of the lake at this camp. They've been hiding the truth about it for years."

"They have?" Lynnette's eyes widened.

"Oh, for sure! They say this lake is haunted."

Without even rolling over, Amber asked, "Who's *they*?"

"I've never heard that before," Kiana sounded worried.

"Maybe they didn't think you could handle it," Carla scoffed.

"Who's *they*?" Amber repeated.

"*They* are the people who know about these things."

"And *they* told you?"

"Of course *they* told me. I'm in their group. We talk about paranormal activity in our chat room."

Amber chided, "An online chat room?"

"Yes."

"And you believed them?"

"Of course I believed them."

"We could like tell the one about the boy who got like chased by a detached hand through an abandoned house," Lynnette offered.

"This doesn't feel good," Kiana said nervously, and curled up with her pillow.

Amber didn't let it drop. "And online, they told you that this little lake in faraway Alaska was haunted?"

"I mentioned it to them because I've heard it before. I bet a lot of lakes up here are haunted. Why not this one?"

Amber rolled over to face Carla. "That's ridiculous! There are over two million lakes in Alaska. If there was all this supernatural stuff going on up here it'd be all over the news, not talked about in a chat room."

"They don't want people to know."

"*They* again!"

A discussion about conspiracy theories went back and forth between Carla and Amber for several minutes. Rinnie zoned it out. She didn't want to hear frightening things and get all creeped out when she was trying to sleep.

She lay on her stomach pulling things out of her backpack. She put on some lip gloss and hand lotion, then decided to select the first secret-sister gift and write a note so it would be ready in the morning.

As she reached into the inside pocket, Rinnie froze. Instead of hearing the crisp plastic store sack crackle, her hand felt a mushy mess. Rinnie was sick! Not the I-ate-too-many-burnt-marshmallows kind of sick, but the I-just-realized-something-horribly-awful kind of sick that twists your stomach, zings your heart, and makes your brain search feverishly for a way to ignore or deny it. She was afraid to look. She didn't dare pull the sack out of the backpack all the way, for fear it would soak her sleeping bag.

"Tell me this isn't true," she whined, as she quickly got down off the bunk to get a towel out of her clothes bag.

"Of course, it's true," Carla snapped. "You gonna argue with me too? I can't believe you're all making such a big deal about it. All I want to do is tell the story involving this camp."

"Leave me out of it," Rinnie said, as she climbed back up.

Carefully, she pulled the drippy, gloppy mess out. The bubbles had leaked—everything was ruined! Rinnie's mind raced to remember what she'd done that could've possibly caused this disaster.

Suddenly she realized what the nagging feeling Sunday night had been about. She'd tried the bubbles in her room and hadn't tightened the lid. After she talked to Nick, she'd forgotten to check it. What was she going to do now? The bubbles were gone. The little blow wand rattled inside the bottle. The candy bar was so gross that she wouldn't even have given it to Carla. The *Friends Stick Together* statue had been next to the dark blue construction paper. It was permanently stained. The sweet angel faces were the bluest of all.

There was hope for the flashlight. Rinnie wiped it off, and turned it on. It worked! Halfway at least. The beam wasn't bright, but it would have to do for the first gift. Now, what would she do about the other three?

Rinnie felt dizzy. Her cabin mates were still arguing.

"What about the really pale girl who like wanted a ride to the dance, and it ended up that she was actually like—dead?" Lynnette asked.

"You're missing the point," Carla fumed.

"Speaking of pale, are you alright?"

As soon as Amber asked Rinnie the question all attention focused on her. She felt overwhelmed and whoozy.

Just then, the door creaked open slowly. The girls were startled.

Cookie glanced around suspiciously. "What's going on here?"

"Cookie! Finally, you're here!" Carla said, in a fake concerned way. "Something's wrong with Rinnie!"

Their leader walked over to see for herself. "Do you need something to eat? I could go get it."

Rinnie's stomach felt all twisted up. The last thing she needed was food. "No, I'm just tired. Thanks anyway."

"You heard her, girls. Get some sleep. Six-thirty comes mighty early, and if six-thirty doesn't suit ya, you can get up at five-thirty when I do, and help with breakfast."

"Good night, Cookie!" they each called out.

"Good night, girls."

It took Rinnie a long time to get to sleep. Her body was worn out, but her mind was frenzied. Mentally, she took inventory of other options she had for secret-sister gifts. She'd bought a candy bar and gum for herself, but one piece of gum was missing and she'd taken a bite out of the candy, so—no help there. Grrr!

No use whining now. She'd just have to deal with it. Think! Think! She'd start with the flashlight, but what about the note with it? The dark blue paper was a soggy blob. She could use the back pages from her journal to write notes on. That would work. Her silver pen was fine. What else did she have? Not much! Rinnie's head throbbed. She wanted to quit thinking, but her brain wouldn't cooperate.

The haunting story crept into her mind. She agreed with Amber that there probably wasn't a conspiracy, but thought there might be some truth to the theory that the event had occurred. Rinnie could hear the loons on the lake. She loved the sound of their plaintive call. Did they know the ghost girl?

Oh brother—what an imagination! she scolded herself. Go to sleep! The loons were just reclaiming their domain. The poor things hid during the day when the girls were splashing around. You couldn't blame them for enjoying some peace and quiet at night.

Still, the loons had been around a long time and might have seen something unusual. Enough! Rinnie touched her triple-heart necklace for comfort, and forced herself to change subjects.

She wondered how her family was doing, and about Nick too—but just as a friend. She thought about Rascal. He was probably chasing magpies off their deck so they wouldn't get into the garbage. Good dog! But knowing him, he'd be getting into the garbage himself. Bad dog! Rinnie missed him. But he'd have been scared to death if he was sleeping at the foot of her bed tonight as he usually did. Cookie snored something fierce. There was no getting away from the racket, so Rinnie started counting: one snore, and two snores, and three snores, and four snores …

Somewhere after thirty-three snores, she finally fell asleep.

Chapter 12

Happy Trails

A rude blast from an air horn awoke the camp on Tuesday morning. Another rude blast sounded five minutes later, in case someone had missed it the first time.

The girls straggled out to the flagpole. They stood quiet and sleepy-eyed in their pajamas. An awesome aroma of food wafted their way from the pavilion. That brought them to attention!

The Juls were raring to go. They took charge of the flag-raising ceremony and led the group in a couple of songs. The leaders appeared tired but determined. One of them said a prayer.

"Good morning, ladies!" Echo echoed. "Today's schedule has been posted at the pavilion, but since most of you aren't awake enough to see it, let me tell you. First-year girls will be having camp certification classes."

There were a couple of cheers.

"Third-years have a service project and a food preparation class with Cookie."

There were a few more cheers, mixed with a couple of groans.

"Yes, you groaners guessed it. Second-year girls get the first hike—a delightful five-mile trek. You'll be leaving at nine o'clock. Be sure to pick up your bag lunch, fill your water bottles, and make all necessary pit stops beforehand. We'll all meet back here this afternoon for volleyball. That's it for now. Have a nice day!"

Rinnie was looking forward to the hike. It was something

she enjoyed doing. Besides that, the long hike would give her a temporary reprieve from the secret-sister gift problem. Who knows, she might even be inspired along the way and figure out what to do.

"Five miles!" Amber griped, as the girls got ready after breakfast. "Is this church camp—or boot camp!"

"What's the matter, Amber, you afraid of a little exercise?" Carla smirked.

Amber was about to verbally explode when one of the Juls showed up to hand out a list of weekly activities. Rinnie resolved to keep those two roommates apart as much as possible.

"Has anybody seen my pink sneakers?"

"You need boots for the hike," Lynnette calmly reminded her.

"I know! But I want my sneakers for later and I can't find them."

"I think you hung them on the bushes to dry yesterday afternoon." Kiana said.

"Yes, I know I hung them on the bushes, but they weren't there this morning." Carla sneered at Amber. "Someone must've taken them. It might have been a joke, but I want them back—now."

Amber walked out of the cabin.

———

The secret sister who had Rinnie's name gave her some bubble gum and a note that read, "May your troubles be like bubbles and pop away." That sounded familiar.

Rinnie's own secret sister was practically invisible. Attendance at the flag ceremony was required. But Rinnie couldn't remember seeing her there, or at breakfast. Later, when Rinnie sneaked down by the other cabins to put the little flashlight in Jessica's mailbox, she hadn't been in her cabin either. What's going on? Rinnie wondered, as she ran to the pavilion to pick up her sack lunch.

Picking up your sack lunch meant making your own peanut butter or ham sandwich, choosing a small bag of potato chips, and grabbing an apple or orange for dessert. It wasn't a lot of food, but adequate nourishment. Girls who had candy usually hid a couple of pieces in their jacket pocket.

Keeping Carla and Amber apart turned out to be easier than Rinnie had anticipated. Amber hadn't attended camp the year before so technically she was a first-year girl. Her hike would be only two miles and not until tomorrow. She gleefully smirked at Carla as the second-year hikers left.

It was a glorious day, the kind that made people glad they lived in Alaska, the kind they looked forward to all winter long. Perfectly formed white clouds floated like sculptures in the brilliantly blue sky. The flowers seemed to vibrate with rich, warm hues, and there were so many shades of green that you couldn't even count them all. The rich, earthy smell that Rinnie loved was everywhere. She took several deep breaths.

Everyone was cheerful. There were things to see, and songs to sing.

Carla and Lynnette moved ahead, visiting with others in the group, which consisted of eight other girls, Dad 1, and Sarge. Kiana wasn't very talkative for some reason, and she kept biting the side of her finger.

Along the way, Rinnie took pictures of a noisy squirrel, a field of dark pink fireweed, a soaring eagle, and a cloud in the shape of an octopus. She planned to give that one to her brother Squid.

She picked a wild rose to smell and study as she walked along. From the texture of the petals down to the structure of the stem, every part was precisely designed for function and beauty. How could anybody who'd ever seen Alaska not believe that there is a God? Rinnie wondered. There were endless mountains, intriguing glaciers, prolific plants, and astonishing animals. Even the bugs were fascinating. Rinnie only had one question, why mosquitoes? They were a pain in the neck—and anywhere else they landed! Several had followed her from the flower area. Once she got rid of them, Rinnie held the flower out to Kiana. "Doesn't this smell heavenly?"

Kiana nodded slightly. She seemed distracted.

"Are you okay?"

"Sure," Kiana said calmly, but she was visibly relieved when it was time for lunch.

Delicate fingers of a spontaneous waterfall cascaded through mountain crevices and created a terraced pool in the area where they ate. Rinnie took a picture of that too, and random pictures of people in the group. A weathered picnic table and several tree stumps served as their dining set. Was it the hiking that made them so hungry, or the fresh air? Either way, it didn't take the group long to devour their lunches.

Kiana still wasn't saying much when the hike resumed, but she began to pause frequently. It wasn't long before the others were ahead of them. They'd gone only another half mile when Kiana sat down on a big, flat rock and started to cry.

"What's going on, Kiana?" Rinnie coaxed.

Between sobs, all Kiana could say was, "My sister's boots—by mistake—too small—big blisters!"

"You poor kid! Here, let me help you get them off." Rinnie nearly lost her lunch when she saw the huge, bloody splotches on Kiana's socks.

"Do you wanna take a picture?" Kiana asked, trying to find humor in a difficult situation.

"No, thanks." Rinnie smiled weakly. What should they do now? Her friend couldn't put the boots back on without excruciating pain. They needed help, but the group was getting farther and farther ahead of them. From the bushes on the path ahead of them came a rustling sound, and then strange, low growls.

"Oh no, what do we do?" Kiana panicked.

"Get large and loud, and see if that scares it off."

"Should I do the loud part or the large part?" Kiana asked, struggling to stand up.

"Both!" Rinnie stood on the rock directly behind Kiana. She raised her arms up as high as possible. "Sing!"

"What?"

"Anything!"

"Old McDonald had a farm E I E I O. And on this farm he had a…"

"Bear!" Carla shouted, as she burst from the bushes, shrieking with laughter.

Kiana's mouth fell open.

Rinnie was ticked. "Of all the dirty rotten—dang you, Carla Clupp!"

"Oh, get over it. Can't you take a joke? The look on your faces was hysterical!"

"Ha ha."

"That's what you get for being so slow."

"We couldn't help it—Kiana has raw, bleeding blisters!"

Carla gazed down at Kiana's injured feet. "Oh, gag! No wonder you couldn't walk anymore."

"Duh! And you guys went on without us!" Rinnie was holding her ground.

"I came back."

"Yeah, to scare us!"

"No, I told them I'd wait down by the stream until you caught up. When you didn't get there, I came looking for you."

Rinnie softened a little. "Oh—thanks. Now that you're here, you and I could link wrists and make a four-handed seat carry."

"Carry *her*? No way! She's bigger than us."

Rinnie was ticked again.

Kiana was embarrassed. "I can walk. I just can't put the boots back on."

"See? She can walk."

Rinnie glared at Carla. "How is she supposed to keep dirt off the wounds?"

"Well, if that's all you're worried about." From out of her jacket pocket, Carla produced a rolled-up pair of clean, dry socks. "I'm always prepared with a spare," she said proudly. "She can wear 'em over the ones she has on until we get back to camp. It'll help."

Rinnie was impressed. "Okay, we have a plan."

Kiana was grateful.

"You're welcome. Just make sure to wash 'em out before you give 'em back to me."

"Sure."

Rinnie rolled her eyes. Carla was a piece of work! But at least it would get them moving ahead again.

Not far down the path, there suddenly came a rustle from the bushes *behind* them. There were low grunting noises.

"Great! Who did you send to scare us now?"

Carla's face went pale. She choked out, "N—nobody!"

"We can't outrun it," Rinnie said. "Time to get large and loud again—hurry!" She and Kiana stood together and raised their arms. "Carla, get over here," Rinnie demanded, and began singing, "Old McDonald had a farm."

"E I E I O," Kiana added.

The rustling got louder. Rinnie turned to face it bravely. "And on this farm there was a …"

Kiana nudged Rinnie to point out that Carla had dropped her water bottle and was running off.

"There was a chicken!" Rinnie shouted in Carla's direction.

"E I E I O," Kiana shouted too.

The noise in the bushes kept getting louder and louder.

"Leave me, Rinnie—go!"

"No way—keep singing!"

A huge moose with massive antlers stepped out onto the path about a hundred feet from the girls. He seemed more annoyed than scared by their tactics, and promptly crossed the path into other bushes.

They each took a deep breath.

Kiana exhaled loudly. "Whoa! Too close for comfort."

"Yeah, we need to get out of here!"

They began walking as fast as Kiana could. A short while later, Carla was there again.

"Wow, I'm glad you guys are okay. I ran ahead to get help."

"Then why didn't they come back with you?"

"Uh—they'll be here soon, I'm sure."

Rinnie and Kiana barely heard her. They were too busy staring at the wet spot on the front of her jeans that ran all the way down her left leg. When Carla realized what they were looking at, her face reddened.

"Dang, I must've spilled my water bottle as I was running."

The other two didn't say anything. Kiana merely handed Carla the water bottle she'd dropped as they walked past her and headed down the path again. They walked for several yards in silence. When they sat down to rest at the stream, they could hear the main group coming back toward them.

"What am I gonna do?" Carla whimpered, mortified.

Rinnie had a flash of brilliance, but knew Carla might not appreciate it. That made it even better. Cupping her hands, Rinnie scooped up a handful of the stream's icy cold water and threw it.

"Are you nuts?" Carla screeched, as the water hit her face and shirt.

"No, she's inspired," Kiana said. Then she scooped up some water and splashed Rinnie, who gasped and splashed her back.

Carla finally caught on. If they were all wet from a water fight, no one would know about her little accident. She splashed even harder. She even splashed herself.

"You girls know better than to get separated from the group!" Sarge scolded, when she arrived on the scene.

"There was a slight problem, so we decided to wait here for you," Rinnie explained.

Sarge took one look at Kiana's feet and started giving orders. Most of the group would go back to camp and Dad 1 would bring back the four-wheeler. Sarge would wait with a few of the others.

While the plan was being implemented, Carla whispered earnestly to Rinnie and Kiana. "Thanks, you guys, for not telling everybody about you-know-what."

"Sure."

"No problem."

"No, I really mean it. *Thanks a lot!*" Carla emphasized. "I will never, never, *never* forget the favor you did for me."

Rinnie gave her a thumbs-up signal. With that, Carla ran off to catch up with the group returning to camp before Kiana could thank her again for the socks.

"Do you really think she'll remember this day forever?" she asked Rinnie.

Rinnie was doubtful. "I think she'll remember it about as long as it takes those pants to dry."

Chapter 13

Knotty Girls

After free time, as they were in the cabin getting ready for dinner, Rinnie asked, "Amber, what did you learn in the classes today?"

"How to be a knotty girl."

"What?" Rinnie, Carla, Lynnette, and Kiana asked at the same time.

Amber burst out laughing. "Calm down, I meant knotty—you know, with a silent k, not naughty as in shame on you! I learned how to tie a bowline knot, a half-hitch knot, a double hitch, and something called a sheet bend or a sheep bend. It wasn't quite clear. Then I made a necklace. As you can see, it's very knotty."

"Oh, brother!" Carla huffed.

"Cute necklace!" Rinnie said. "The beads are neat too."

"It's like way cool," Lynnette added.

"Did you tie knots all day?" Kiana asked.

"No, I learned how to make a fire too, and to recognize different types of clouds, but that was *knot* as fun."

"Okay, we get it. Quit saying *knot*," Carla grouched.

"I think *knot*," Amber smirked.

"That's it—I'm outta here!" Carla said, and grabbed her jacket. "Ready, Lynnette?"

Lynnette smiled, mischievously. "*Knot* yet."

Carla tossed her head in disgust and left.

Rinnie raised an eyebrow. "You shouldn't tease her so much. She might decide to get even."

"Ooh, I'm really afraid of her—*knot!* She already thinks I stole her dumb sneakers. I see the looks she gives me."

"Well, did you?" Rinnie asked, jokingly.

"Knot on your life! They're pukey pink. Gag! Now, if they'd been black ..."

"I didn't take them either. Did you, Lynnette?"

"*Knot* likely."

Kiana said, "I still think she left them out all night and some animal got them."

Amber pretended to scowl. "Silly critters! Don't they know you're not supposed to wear sneakers with fur?"

While cabin C reverberated with laughter and conversation, Carla had a heart-to-heart chat with Echo.

That night, as the group gathered by the campfire dodging mosquitoes and random raindrops, Echo announced, "We had a superb day today and hope we can continue the camp spirit into tomorrow. Just a couple of reminders—I'm still seeing wrappers around from the candy and gum that weren't invited to camp. Please be more conscientious about your cleanups. Also, someone is missing a pair of pink sneakers. Everyone please keep an eye out for them, and if you 'borrowed' them, please return them immediately.

"One more thing, we had a random act of kindness displayed today on the second-years' hike. Two girls were having trouble keeping up, and someone else—I won't name names—stayed behind to help them. That's the kind of friendship we like to see."

Rinnie whispered to Kiana. "Do you think Carla told Echo the *whole* hike story?"

Kiana shook her head. "*Knot* in a million years!"

It's often said that if you don't like the weather in Alaska, wait five minutes and it'll change. It did—it got worse! When the random raindrops turned into drizzle, they toughed it out because they wanted to make s'mores. When the drizzle turned into a downpour, all scrambled for the cabins.

Chapter 14

Wednesday Woes

The call of nature woke Rinnie up early on Wednesday morning. What time was it? Rinnie rolled over and tried to guess by peering through a space in the ill-fitting cotton curtains. No luck. It was almost dark, and the only way you got a dark morning during an Alaska summer was if it was completely overcast and stormy. Even then, it wasn't dark-dark, just a wide variety of grays. Bummer! It would be a muddy mess wherever they went, and the mosquitoes would get feistier.

That wasn't the worst of Rinnie's woes. She needed to come up with another secret-sister gift somehow. But what? Again, she scolded herself for biting into her candy bar on the way to camp. It would be too obvious if she cut around the teeth marks and used that. It wasn't like she could use any of the secret-sister gifts that she might receive either, because she wasn't sure who *her* secret sister was. It might even be Jessica. In that case, it would be like saying, "Oh, I thought so much of you that I decided to give *you* something you brought for *me*." Nope, that wouldn't work at all. What was she going to do? Her brain was baffled.

Her bladder kept vying for attention too. She grew more uncomfortable by the minute, but oh, how she dreaded the porta-potty dash! An outhouse would be closer, but it would be extra dark in there, and she didn't have a flashlight. Besides, technically she wasn't supposed to go outside alone at night, for safety reasons. But technically it wasn't nighttime. Rinnie hated to wake someone up to go with her. None of them would be thrilled to leave a warm sleeping bag to go running out in the rain. They were all zonked. It looked like a mouth-breathers convention. How they could sleep through the snare drum solo that the heavy rain was playing on the cabin's old tin roof was beyond her.

Still, there was no use avoiding it. She could probably get there and back before anyone noticed. Rinnie quietly slipped off the bunk and put on her shoes and hooded sweatshirt.

Cookie's travel alarm clock buzzed as she got to the door.

"Where are you going?" the leader asked, groggily.

Rinnie shifted from one foot to the other and sent a very distressed look in her leader's direction. She didn't need to say anything else.

"Okay. Hang on. I'm coming."

Rinnie decided to wait on the porch while Cookie got dressed. The lifeless campground was shrouded in dismal gloom. It wasn't hard to imagine that the place might be haunted. The mist that veiled the lake seemed like a portal to another world. A forlorn feeling crept over Rinnie, followed by goose bumps once again.

"Ready?"

Rinnie jumped. "Oh—yeah—sure." The immediate need once more caught her attention. She was glad that Cookie was a fast dresser. Cookie was also a fast dasher and almost beat Rinnie to the potties. Thank heavens there was more than one!

Disinfectant hand gel and baby wipes were available but that wasn't thorough enough for Cookie. Anyone who came near the cooking area in the pavilion had to perform rigorous hand scrubbing. She had a specific area set up for that. There was even a wooden plaque that read: "The only good germ is a dead germ." After all, she hadn't planned healthy, balanced menus, and purchased precise amounts of groceries just to have it ruined by microbic mischief.

After Rinnie had washed properly, she asked if there was anything she could do to help.

"Sure, why don't you cut the cantaloupe?"

While Rinnie started the task, Cookie got the massive

six-burner propane stoves all fired up. She started one pan with bacon, and one with sausage, set two huge kettles full of water on to heat up for the instant oatmeal or hot chocolate, and started cracking eggs to scramble. Everything was perfectly organized. The cooking area was inside a large tent with mesh sides that let smoke and tantalizing smells out, and kept frustrated mosquitoes from getting in. Rinnie watched, fascinated, and temporarily forgot about the rain.

As Cookie worked, she sang or talked to herself. The pavilion was far enough away from the cabins that no one could hear what was being said or if songs were off-key. Cookie was glad to visit while she worked, but she seldom looked directly at the person she was talking to. Her off-set eyes were hard to follow. People were never quite sure which one was looking at them, but it didn't appear to shake her confidence any.

Cookie handed Rinnie a cup of hot chocolate as soon as it was ready. "I've been watching you," she said, and began to whisk through a huge pan of eggs. "You don't seem too happy. Homesick or heartsick?"

"A little of both."

"What are you sad about?" Cookie asked, handing Rinnie a turner to flip pancakes with while they talked. "Come on, spit it out!"

Rinnie tried not to cry. She choked back the emotional lump. There'd been plenty of disappointments. Her friend, Erica, wasn't there. The gift stuff was ruined, and the stress level in the cabin was awful. But how could she tell Cookie without it looking like she was dogging on Carla?

Rinnie decided to go straight to the biggest problem. "First I need to tell you a story." She proceeded to explain how her perfect secret-sister gift plan had failed. When she'd finished explaining and had flipped most of the pancakes, Rinnie sighed heavily.

"So, what are you going to do about it?"

Rinnie shrugged.

"Did you keep the bubble bottle?"

"Yeah."

"That's an easy fix. Bring it over here after breakfast. We'll put some dish detergent and water in it—and voila!"

"Really?"

"Sure. People made bubbles that way for years before you could ever buy them from a store."

"Cool!" Rinnie was excited. It was so simple. "But what am I gonna do about tomorrow and the next day?"

"You'll think of something. The secret-sister thing is meant to add to the fun, not drive you nuts. Be imaginative. A gift means more if it means something to the giver."

"I'll keep working on it."

"Atta girl! Now tell me, how are things going with Carla?"

Rinnie stammered. "It's not easy to find words. I mean, she's basically a good person, you know, but … uh …"

"She's a brat," Cookie finished Rinnie's sentence.

Rinnie protested, "I never said that."

"No, I did. I know what she's like. Some people have no clue that there are other people on the planet who have feelings. They tend to learn things the hard way. But what can you do? If you're related, you gotta love 'em."

"I have a big brother like that. He's so frustrating."

"Yup. Sometimes the hardest people to love are the ones who need it the most. If things get out of hand, tell me and I'll have a talk with her."

Rinnie didn't have the heart to tell Cookie that things already had. She decided to try harder to get along with Carla before she called for backup.

The sun peeked through the clouds momentarily, and the rain subsided. A sunny break, some people call it. Whatever it was called, it was magnificent. The rain dripping off the pavilion eaves caught the sunbeams and glistened like golden honey. Rinnie was awed by the sight of it.

The shy loons came out from hiding and enthusiastically called to each other as they bobbed and danced around the lake. Other birds joined in, creating a symphony of trills, chirps, and quacks.

Cookie stopped for a minute to enjoy the splendor. "Amazing isn't it? I often witness incredible things when I'm out here early in the morning."

"It's such a simple thing too—the sun shining through raindrops, but it's gorgeous, and the birds love it!"

"They sure do. I hope it lasts."

"Me too!" Rinnie added. In the next second she nearly jumped out of her skin.

Dad 2 had sounded the wake-up call. That air horn blasted longer and louder than any Rinnie had ever heard.

"If that doesn't wake 'em up, nothing will!" Cookie chuckled. "Tell them to dress warm. Bring that bubble bottle back and we'll get it taken care of."

"Thanks so much, Cookie!"

The horn sounded again. Rinnie held her hands over her ears and ran.

———————

As soon as everyone was assembled at the flagpole, the wind kicked up, forcing menacing clouds in front of the sun. The leaders decided against putting the flag up right then, and sent everyone off to meet under the pavilion instead. The rain started again, and came down hard. After breakfast, the girls were told to scurry back to their cabins and use the morning to work on their skits.

Rinnie stayed behind to make more bubble broth.

"So, who's this for?" Cookie asked. "You can trust me not to tell."

"Jessica Jeffries."

"Now there's a story!"

"I've heard that, but no one has told me what it is."

"Are you asking the right questions?"

"Apparently not. All I know is that she's the shyest girl I've ever met in my life. I never see her talking to anybody. I don't see her out and about anywhere, and if she's around someone, she practically hides behind them. What's going on with her?"

Cookie sat down and calmly said. "She spends a lot of time talking to leaders in the first-aid cabin."

"Is she sick?"

"Yes and no. Her affliction is called grief. Jessica is reacting normally for someone whose life has been torn apart."

"Torn apart? What do you mean?"

"Two months ago she lived back east in a comfortable house with two wonderful parents. Then it was all gone. One night they were killed in a car accident, and shortly afterwards she had to leave everything behind that was familiar and secure to her and move thousands of miles away to Alaska to live with an aunt and uncle she barely knows."

"You're kidding! How awful!"

"Yes, it's terrible. Imagine how you'd deal with that."

Rinnie's mind raced. What if *her* mom and dad were gone all of a sudden? What if she lost everything and was sent away to live with strangers? She felt sick even thinking about it.

They sat quietly for a moment, then Rinnie said, "I'm surprised she came to camp."

"They *sent* her, hoping that it might help her make a few friends before the school year started and she had to face two thousand other kids."

"Oh. Good idea. I want to be her friend, but it's hard to get close to her." Rinnie cringed inside. It was only partly true. She'd been watching Jessica from a distance instead of reaching out to her with more than little secret-sister gifts.

"Keep trying. Now that you know her story, do you see her differently?"

Rinnie nodded.

"Hey, I know you can handle this. You're a good kid."

Rinnie grinned halfheartedly. She knew she could do better. But what about the secret-sister gifts? What would Jessica think if she didn't receive anything else because Rinnie had nothing to give? Feeling more pressured than ever, Rinnie ran back to the cabin.

Chapter 15

A Haunting Tale

The atmosphere at the cabin didn't help. There was a big argument going on.

"Oh, Rinnie, glad you're here. We need your vote. They said we should like work on our skit. Will you like listen to my idea for a minute?"

"Sure, what is it?" Rinnie asked.

"We can do that anytime. We've got a massively dreary day. It's perfect for telling ghost stories," Carla insisted.

"What's with you and ghost stories?" Amber asked.

"I think they're fascinating. Don't you?"

"*Knot* really."

"Don't start that again."

Changing the subject, Kiana asked, "So, what's your idea, Lynnette?"

"I think we should like use the music to *America the Beautiful* and change the words, so instead of like 'from sea to shining sea' it could like be about us, because our names all start with c, and it could be like 'from C to shining C.' Okay?"

"Yeah."

"Sounds cool."

Rinnie and Kiana tried to pay attention, but it was difficult, especially when Carla and Amber were verbally jousting.

"I still think we should tell stories."

Rinnie tried extra hard to be patient with Carla. "We really need to get this other thing done. Maybe later …"

"You just don't want to hear a story because it's not about *you*."

"What?"

"I read about you in the newspaper—Miss Save-the-Neighbor-from-a-Crazy-Person!"

Rinnie's jaw tightened and her fist clenched. She was trying not to deck this girl, but she was so tempted to scream, "You have no clue what I went through *before* that article was written!" Instead, she forced herself to smile. "How about this? You can tell one story, then we'll work on the skit until it's ready. Everyone fine with that?"

They all agreed.

"Alright!" Carla clapped.

Amber rolled her eyes. "Oh, joy."

"I'm gonna like jot stuff down while we're waiting."

"Don't you want to listen, Lynnette?"

"I can pay attention and like write at the same time."

Kiana said, "Come over to my bunk, Lynnette, and I'll help. Scary stories and me don't mix."

Carla's face twisted impatiently. "Is anyone going to listen, or not?"

Rinnie shook her head at Amber so she wouldn't say *knot* and aggravate the situation further. Amber went along with appeasing Carla—for the moment.

"Okay, there was this girl, about our age, and she lived in one of these cabins with her family."

"She must've had a tiny family," Amber snickered.

"Cut it out and listen!"

"Okay. Go!"

"Fine. One night she needed to go to the outhouse, which was farther away from the cabin than the ones here, and it was in the winter on the darkest and foggiest night of the year." Carla paused to see if Rinnie and Amber were getting the spookiness of it.

Rinnie tried to ignore the goose bumps that had crept up on her once more, and appear interested in the tale. Amber tried to keep a straight face.

"So, like I said, it was very dark—clouds covered the moon, and the fog was so thick she could hardly breathe. The only light she had was a candle …"

"She took an open flame into an outhouse? That's brave!" Rinnie cleared her throat.

Amber whispered, "Sorry!"

Carla forged on. "Anyway ... she only had a candle, but as she was walking along, the flame suddenly died! She got confused and didn't know what direction to go in. She searched and searched, but she couldn't find her way back to the cabin."

"I remember this story now," Lynnette whispered to Kiana. They quit brainstorming and were listening now.

Carla loved the attention. She continued, sounding as mysterious as possible. "Eventually the poor girl wandered down by the lake and slipped on the snow-covered grass, tumbled down the bank, and fell into the freezing cold lake. She tried to get back to the shore, but her heavy flannel nightgown weighed her down. When she became too tired to fight and hypothermia set in, she slipped beneath the deep, dark water and *drowned!*

"When they realized she was missing the next morning, they looked high and low for her. The only clue that was found was in a bush by the lake. The blue hair ribbon from her braided hair was caught in the brambles and waved hauntingly in the breeze.

"To this day, they say her ghost wanders at night, trying to find its way back to the cabin. We might see her roaming *tonight!*"

Rinnie was certain this tale wasn't true, but there was something about it that got to her every time ... and Carla *had* done a credibly dramatic job. Still, they needed to move on.

"Thanks for the story," Rinnie said.

"Wait a minute," Amber said, "I have a problem with it. First of all, where the heck were the girl's parents?"

"What?"

"I mean, it was supposed to be in one of these cabins, right?"

"Yes, it was," Carla answered smugly.

"Well, look how small they are. You don't think they'd notice if somebody was missing?"

"It was at night. They were asleep."

"Have you ever tried to sneak out at night? My parents hear me and we have a two-story house."

"She wasn't sneaking."

"I know. So she would've made a normal amount of noise, and *normal* is louder than *sneaky*," Amber insisted.

"You're missing the point. I'm trying to explain why this place is haunted," Carla protested.

Amber didn't let up. "The second problem is, did they know where she was only because of a ribbon blowing in the breeze? I mean, couldn't they see a body floating in the lake?"

"Oh—no, because it was like winter and there was like a thin layer of ice all over the lake and she was in there until like spring," Lynnette interjected.

"Yes, yes, there was ice—all over," Carla nodded. "I forgot that part. She was weighed down by her coat and her heavy flannel night gown."

Kiana frowned sympathetically. "Poor girl. Did she at least make it to the outhouse first?"

"Alrighty then," Rinnie tried to change the subject once more.

Amber jumped in again. "Oh, she made it to the outhouse. She probably found her way to it by the smell. But if she'd called her parents from the outhouse and got directions, none of this would have ever happened."

"What? Called her parents? It was an outhouse, not a phone booth!" Carla snapped.

"I know. But, if she'd had a cell phone she could've said, 'Mom, Dad, this is Lula Belle. If you were in the outhouse right now, which way would you head to get back to the cabin?'"

Carla bristled. "Cell phones weren't invented yet!"

"Now *that's* the tragic part of the story." Amber declared.

Rinnie hurriedly added, "Okay—time to work on the skit!"

Working on the skit didn't go well. Carla wouldn't agree to anything that Lynnette and Kiana had come up with. Did she have a better suggestion? No. It was maddening!

Rinnie had clenched her teeth so hard her head hurt.

Lynnette cried and said she wanted to move to a different cabin. Kiana nearly chewed off the side of her finger, and Amber put a pillow over her head and started loudly singing *Ninety-Nine Bottles of Beer on the Wall*. Finally, it was lunchtime—thank heavens!

Chapter 16

Rainy Day Games

It was still raining after lunch. The Juls got everyone involved in playing games. The first one was called Fruit Salad. The girls formed a big circle under the pavilion, or as close to a circle as they could make without half of them sticking out in the rain. They sounded off—one, two, three, one two, three … all around the circle. The ones were apples. The twos were oranges, and the threes were bananas. A girl stood in the center and called out one of the fruit names—for instance, *apples*. Each person who was an apple had to trade places with another apple person before the girl in the center took her spot. The girl without a place had to stand in the center and call out another fruit name, and then those people had to move. But she could also say, "Fruit Salad!" and everyone had to move at least two places. That part got chaotic—girls dashing every which way.

It worked better if people had chairs to sit on than it did with people standing, but regardless, Rinnie was glad they tried it. She wasn't eager to go back to the cabin. She was tired of refereeing between bunkmates. She'd been determined to get along with Carla, but it was exhausting. The girl made it so difficult. So, although the fruit salad game was old-fashioned and not exactly meant to be played under a pavilion in the rain, it was a welcome relief, and exercise.

Next, the Juls introduced an Alaska trivia game. Each cabin was a team. Each team received a paper numbered from one to ten. The group that got the most right answers would win a delicious treat. The Juls took turns asking the questions.

"Question one: What is the correct term for a moose rack?"

"Horns!" Kiana said, quickly.

Amber whispered. "No—wait—antlers!"

The rest of the girls agreed, and Lynnette wrote down *antlers*.

"Question two: What is the state gem?"

"Gold!" Carla said out loud. Other teams began to write it down.

"Wait," Rinnie whispered. "The gem is jade. The mineral is gold."

Lynnette wrote it down.

"Question three: What is the state tree?"

"I got that one," Carla whispered, "Spruce."

"Question four: What is the state flower?"

"Fireweed!" Carla again.

Amber corrected her. "No, it's the forget-me-not," she said, but smiled as she did so Carla didn't get offended.

"Question five: What in Alaska is twenty thousand, three hundred and twenty feet tall?"

"Mount McKinley!" everyone said in unison. Alaska was dang proud of that mountain so most school kids knew the number.

Cabin C worked together to get the answers for state fish: king salmon; and state fossil: woolly mammoth. Some people kidded around about the state bird being the mosquito, but they knew it was really the willow ptarmigan.

"It's tarmigan," Carla declared, looking over Lynnette's shoulder.

Rinnie whispered, "Yeah, but remember, it's got that silent *P* on the front."

Carla grinned and bobbled her head, "Oh, duh—sorry!"

"No problem." Rinnie was glad they were finally getting along.

The state sport was easy: dog mushing. But number ten was tricky.

"What is the state motto?"

"North to Alaska!"

"No." Lynnette said.

"Land of the Midnight Sun."

"No!" Lynnette said, stubbornly and put the pencil down. "I *really* like *have* this one. You gotta like trust me, okay?" Lynnette proudly wrote down, *North to the Future.*

In the end, the cabin C team got nine and a half points. Technically the state tree was a Sitka spruce, so they got only half a point for that one, but it was enough to win an Alaska flag sticker, and the right to be the first ones in line for the Dutch oven brownies that Cookie had made. The prize wasn't much, but the brownies were scrumptious, and the teamwork was priceless. Another nice thing happened. Before the brownies were completely devoured, the rain stopped.

"Volleyball!" the Juls cried out, and everyone ran out into the field.

As Rinnie was waiting on the sidelines for a chance to get into the game, she saw something interesting. Jessica was sitting on Ponder Rock blowing bubbles.

Volleyball after a rainstorm was a muddy mess, and so were the girls who played it. Getting cleaned up for dinner became a priority. Rinnie was glad she'd brought an extra kitchen garbage bag to put dirty things in. There wasn't any room left on the porch railing to hang things. The others had beaten her to it. Her stuff could wait until it got home. Her hair was getting unbearably gross though, and she couldn't wait to wash it. For now, she'd have to put the hankie back on it, or a hat.

Other than her hair, things were looking up. In Rinnie's mailbox was a neat pen and an eight-inch notebook with daisies on it. There was a message that read: "A friend like you is "write on!" Cute. She decided to use the notebook for a special project, and let her mind wander through some of the possibilities. It was a stall tactic. Rinnie was avoiding making a decision about what to give Jessica on Thursday.

The mood in the cabin had improved. They even talked

about the skit and set up a practice time before Thursday night. It wouldn't be an Academy-Award-winning performance, but it would do. Lynnette was pleased. Carla even cooperated. It was like a miracle—while it lasted.

"The skit's missing one thing though," Amber pretended to critique. "You should've put something in there about snow snakes."

"Snow snakes?"

"Yeah, you know, those slithery skiffs that blow across roads in the winter ahead of cars."

"You mean like squiggly snow drifts?" Lynnette smiled. She didn't get offended. She knew Amber was playing.

"That's what they want you to think, but no, they're snow snakes. They hibernate in the summer down by the permafrost and come out only in the wintertime."

"They're related to ice worms," Rinnie joined in the jest.

"Yes, I forgot that part, and scientists don't want to tell you, but it's the ice worms that made those deep holes in the glaciers. In the time of the mammoths they were as huge as …"

"Anacondas!" Rinnie called out.

"That's it, anacondas, and they burrowed deep into the ice fields and made crevices for people to fall into."

"And crevasses."

"Both."

"Don't be stupid. Ice worms are microscopic!" Carla said, with a curious look.

"That's their babies. Wait until they grow up!" Kiana giggled.

"Very funny!" Carla was indignant. Her nose wrinkled as though smelling stench, and she said to Kiana, "I liked it better when you were invisible."

"As invisible as snow snakes?" Kiana giggled louder.

Carla glared at her.

"Oh, come on," Amber kidded. "We're just goofing around. Too much sugar in those brownies, I guess. But, hey, wasn't it as good as your ghost story—maybe even a little more creative?"

"As if …"

Amber mock-sighed, "Oh well, we tried."

Carla's eyes narrowed. "If you're so creative, why don't you tell me the story of where you hid my pink sneakers?"

All the smiles faded, especially Amber's. The two girls locked stares. Rinnie was getting ready to jump between them in case hair started to fly.

However, Amber stayed calm. "Have you checked in all the outhouses?"

Carla stomped her foot. "That's disgusting!" She left in a huff and slammed the door behind her.

Rinnie turned to Amber, with a scolding grin. "You know she's gonna go look in all those old, smelly buildings, don't ya?"

Lynnette was concerned. "Did you really like put her shoes down one of them?"

"No. I never said that I took her shoes, or that I put them anywhere. I just asked her if she'd checked in all the outhouses."

"Here we go again!" Rinnie said. But actually, the more she thought about it, Amber was right. Believing there was a ghost at Camp Kachemak made about as much sense as believing in snow snakes. She wasn't going to waste another minute worrying about it.

Chapter 17

Tissue Issues

Wednesday night, Echo said, "It's been an extraordinary day today. We learned that when we're in the domain of Mother Nature, we have to be flexible. There are things that we didn't get done as planned, but we'll work on them tomorrow. Please be sure to check the new schedule of events at the pavilion bright and early.

"We have a special campfire planned for tonight. Because of that, there won't be many announcements—just a couple of things. Booger the bear has been spotted in our area again."

There were several gasps.

"No need to panic, just be watchful and wary. He tore up a campground not far from here while the people were fishing. Let's be careful with what we leave around, especially food-related items, and above all, don't go off on your own, for any reason! Now, our last item of business is: The pink sneakers are still missing and the owner would *sure* like to have them back. Let's work together on this, ladies. Thank you."

Someone called out, "Maybe Booger bear took 'em."

Echo ignored the remark and the program proceeded. It was a solemn occasion.

Each leader presented a spiritual story or poem, and the meeting concluded with the Juls singing, *How Great Thou Art.* The girls were each given a pocket-sized pack of tissues and a letter from home that they were to read in a quiet moment back in their cabins.

Right away, Rinnie recognized the envelope that was

handed to her. It belonged to the card her mom had been so determined to find at the store. The first tissue was used up before she even got back to her bunk. Tears trickled down her cheeks as she read.

Dear Rinnie,

I hope you're having a terrific time. I miss you! But I'm glad that you have this opportunity to get away and have some fun. My, what a summer it's been! It was so nice to go shopping with you the other day. Thank you for making me take a break.

We get so busy that sometimes we forget to spend time together, or say meaningful things to each other. I'm glad that I had this chance to express what I feel in my heart.

Do you know how wonderful you are? Do you know how much you're loved? Very! My darling girl, please never doubt it!

I'm proud of you, and of the choices that you're making in life. You will go far if you continue to do what's right and fair. I know it's tough nowadays, but hang in there, kiddo! You are stronger and wiser than you realize, but you don't have to do it alone. Dad and I are here for you—talk to us!

We can't always afford the best of things, but it's not because you don't deserve them—you do! So I'm sending the best of my love in the best card I could find, along with a huge hug in this envelope.

Sleep tight. Love you tons—always—Mom.

Rinnie wept into her pillow. She missed her mother. She missed her dad. She missed her bed. And she was out of tissues! It was an overwhelming sensation of misery, but she wasn't alone. Other girls were sniffling too. It was a relief to boo-hoo out loud and vent it all.

When the cabin got quiet, Carla exhaled noisily, and said,

"It's about time! What a bunch of babies! Can we get on to something fun—like telling more ghost stories? I've got some that will scare the socks off you."

"Just what we need after a tender moment!" Amber replied sarcastically.

"Can't you go to sleep?" Rinnie pleaded.

"Sleep? Aren't we were going to hang out?"

"We've been hanging out all day." Kiana mumbled.

Lynnette murmured, "Some peace and quiet would be like so nice."

"You guys are a drag!"

Amber warned, "Don't even go there unless you want to hear something you won't like."

"Oh, really? And what would that be?"

"See if you can figure it out. Good night."

"Good night."

"Good night."

"Good night."

"You guys are rude!"

No one responded. They all knew silence would bug Carla more than continuing to argue.

When the cabin was quiet again, a timid voice asked, "Does anyone have another pillowcase?"

Everyone cracked up laughing.

Chapter 18

Test of Friendship

After the flag ceremony on Thursday morning, Echo peered around the circle at the pajamaed participants, and then made a sobering announcement. "An incident of tremendous concern occurred early this morning. When two of the Juls were going to the porta-potties, they saw someone in a nightgown wandering by the lake alone. When they went to warn her that she shouldn't be out there, she was nowhere to be found."

Carla gave her cabin mates an I-told-you-so smirk.

"Now, girls, the rules against being out alone are very strict, and for good reason—personal safety. Obviously whoever did this knew she wasn't supposed to be out because she hid from the Juls, making the situation even more perilous. It must not happen again!"

Carla raised her hand. "Are they sure it wasn't a ghost?"

"That's not funny. We're trying to be serious now. I will talk with you later, young lady!"

While they were getting dressed, Lynnette, Kiana, and Amber talked about the possible appearance of an apparition. The uneasiness could be felt throughout the cabin. Rinnie remained quiet.

"Can you believe that?" Amber asked, when the other two had gone to breakfast.

Rinnie shook her head. "I don't want to."

There wasn't much choice on Thursday morning. The only thing Rinnie could think to give Jessica was her new T-shirt. Luckily, she hadn't worn it yet! She tore another piece of paper from the back of her journal, and wrote down a rhyme she'd concocted during breakfast. "Hope this suits you to a T. Your friendship means a lot to me. If you're my friend, I'll happy be!" It was a stretch—but it rhymed!

Rinnie hesitated to leave the cabin after she put her pen away. Glancing around the room, a not-so-friendly idea crossed her mind. What if Amber *had* taken Carla's shoes? It wasn't like Amber wanted them. Maybe it was a prank that went bad. Rinnie was so tired of hearing Carla whine about it that she was tempted to look through Amber's things just to be certain. If Rinnie found the shoes, she could help bring about a graceful ending. Looking would be easy, and who would ever know?

Rinnie walked toward Amber's bunk, and then stopped. "I can't believe you're even thinking this," she said, aloud, and marched herself out of there—pronto!

Most of Thursday was spent finishing camp certification classes and hikes. Rinnie still needed to go to the axe-sharpening and knife safety class, as well as pass her orienteering skills. She had her own compass, and if she showed a leader that she already knew how to use it, she could skip orienteering and go to the Dutch oven cooking class that Cookie was presenting—something she really wanted to do.

Amber didn't get out of going on a hike after all. But she was upbeat. Rinnie saw her hanging out with the other first-year girls who were gathering, and could hear her making witty comments that made everyone laugh. Rinnie was mad at herself for doubting Amber—even for a second.

Immediately after lunch the second-year girls were supposed to do a service project. Some of them put on gloves and disinfected the porta-potties. Some of them helped Cookie prepare things for dinner. Rinnie's cabin was supposed to gather kindling and stack firewood that Dad 1 was busy chopping for the next two nights' campfires. Lynnette went to help Snip and Snap with the award scrolls that were to be given out on the last night. That left Carla, Kiana, and Rinnie for the task.

"Why do we always get stuck with the dirty jobs?" Carla grumbled.

"I'd rather do this than clean potties," Rinnie said, as she unloaded an armful of kindling.

"Yeah, but they'll be done faster."

Rinnie knew it was useless to argue, so she kept stacking.

A short time later, Amber was back from her hike and pitched in to help them. She started telling about all the nature stuff she'd seen, who she met, and who threw up their lunch. Kiana and Rinnie laughed. Carla was surprisingly quiet.

Amber hadn't been back too long when Echo and Sarge pulled her aside to talk. The other girls made as little noise as possible so they could overhear.

In an apologetic tone, Echo said, "It's been mentioned to us that you may be the one hiding the missing shoes. Is it true?"

Amber was stunned. "I give up!" she whimpered, and ran toward the lake. Echo called for her to come back and talk to them, but she didn't.

Rinnie carried a few more logs over by the fire pit, and left to follow Amber. That made Carla mad. Kiana started to leave too, heading in the direction of the leaders. That made Carla *extra* mad.

"Where do you think you're going?" she snarled. "You can't leave me here to do all the work!"

Rinnie was about to say something, when Kiana bravely spouted, "What's the matter, Carla, you afraid of a little exercise? Get your ghost buddy to help ya."

———

Amber was sitting on the old boat launch throwing

slivers of the splintered wood into the water. Rinnie could tell she'd been crying.

Without even looking up, Amber asked, "Did they send you out to fetch the weirdo?"

"No. I came because I wanted to."

"Why bother?"

"Because you're my friend."

Amber scoffed. "I didn't think you still considered me a friend. It's not like we ever hang out anymore."

"We've hung out this week."

Amber grinned. "Yeah, we were the knotty girls."

"Yup, and not everyone appreciated it."

"Who cares? Some people need to lighten up."

"Agreed! Anyway, Carla got stuck stacking wood all by herself." Rinnie then repeated what Kiana had said.

"Good for her!"

The girls sat quietly for a few moments. Rinnie had hoped telling about what Kiana had said would cheer Amber up. But it hadn't quite, so Rinnie tried to relieve the nervous tension another way. "Okay, here's a riddle for you—what do you get from a silly rope?"

Amber groaned. "I can already tell this is gonna be bad. What?"

"Knot knot jokes!"

"That's terrible. I wish I'd come up with it."

"It's all yours."

"Gee, thanks," Amber almost smiled, but then got quiet again. "Did you hear what they asked me?"

"Yeah."

"Blame everything on the Goth girl!"

"No."

"Yes! Apparently Carla told them I stole her shoes, so they asked. I've tried hard to fit in all week, and for what? Their opinion of me will never change. I'm ready to go home." Amber started to cry again.

Rinnie was mad. A rumor could cause such damage. Grr! Yet, after her own doubting episode, she couldn't fault the leaders for wondering. Carla had pestered everybody all week long about those dang sneakers. Echo probably *had* to check into it. Rinnie didn't think they'd deliberately hurt Amber's feelings, but Amber didn't know them well enough to realize that. How could Rinnie help her understand?

She couldn't. The leaders would have to fix this somehow. The only thing Rinnie could do was change the subject. She kidded, "If you go home, the camp ghost will get me."

Amber sniffed. "I'd never believe anything Carla says, but I have to admit, hearing about what the Juls saw this morning was spooky—even for me."

"I think Carla's told the story to too many people, or the Juls didn't have their contacts in right. I refuse to be psyched out anymore."

Rinnie glanced around the dock. It gave her an idea. "Hey, grab a canoe. I'll get the life jackets!"

Amber sniffled loudly. "You're on!"

Chapter 19

The Rescue

It was a dazzling day and the sun felt marvelous after the drenching they'd had on Wednesday. Rinnie and Amber wanted to enjoy it while they could. Before long the other girls would be finished with their tasks and want a turn with the boat.

The lake at Camp Kachemak was ringed by thick stands of trees—a mixture of pine and birch—that grew right to the edge of a four-foot embankment on all but the camp side. The contrast between the natural wild growth and the cleared area of camp gave the place a sense of serenity. When they reached the center of the lake the girls decided to drift and relax.

Rinnie took a deep breath. "I love the smell after rain. Everything's so clean."

"Except for the muddy places," Amber noted sarcastically, as she made ripples through the water with her hand.

"Okay, true. But the trees smell heavenly." She was trying to get the nerve to ask a question.

"What are you thinking about?"

Rinnie felt self-conscious. "It's a dumb question."

"Go for it."

"Okay. Does a nose ring hurt all the time? It's such a sensitive area. Did it take a long time to heal? I got one piercing in my ears, and it took my ears forever."

"Were you using alcohol on them?"

"Sometimes."

"That's why. It affects how fast they heal."

"I didn't know that."

"And no, a nose ring doesn't hurt all the time, but it was sure gross when I had a cold a few weeks ago. I woke up with snot caked all over it. Now that hurt!"

"Oh, sick!"

"You know it! It took me an hour with warm water and a wash cloth to get it all loosened up and cleaned off. Boy, did it pull!"

"Ouch! It wouldn't be worth it to me—to go through all that."

"It's worth it to me."

"Why?" Rinnie blurted out, earnestly. "And what's with the black hair? I always wanted to have hair your color, and now—I mean, yuck!" She winced, afraid of the reaction. She wasn't trying to be nasty. She truly didn't get it.

Amber started paddling angrily. "You're just like the other churchy girls! You think I'm evil. I should've known!"

"Hey, I'm not picking on you. I'm trying to understand how someone I thought I knew could change so drastically, that's all. So, cut out the churchy-girl talk."

"Why? I see the way your group looks at me when I walk down the hall at school. I hear them whispering."

"Well, guess what? I get the same from your group too—so there!" Rinnie snapped back loudly, wobbling her head with attitude.

Amber giggle-snorted. "Don't do that—please! You look like Carla when you do."

Rinnie gasped, "That's scary—thanks for warning me!"

The tension eased.

A small plane circled over the lake twice. The second time it came awfully close to the tree tops on the north end of the lake. The engine was sputtering.

Rinnie looked up. "That sounds bad."

"For sure," Amber agreed.

The plane gained momentum again and flew out of sight.

Amber sighed. "Rinnie, you know me. I'm not evil. I'm just doing something different. It's kinda like Halloween every day—spooks people and bugs my parents. But it's good for them."

"It is?"

"Yeah, they used to yell at each other all the time—almost got a divorce. Now they're having deep conversations about where they went wrong and what they need to do. It's a lot calmer at home."

"That's why you did it?"

"Not entirely. It's just a nice side benefit. I've been a straight-arrow kid for years, and it got me nowhere. My brother's been in lots of trouble, and they were giving him anything he wanted if he'd go to rehab. He went twice! I guess you could say I finally learned how to work the system. That's why I agreed to come to camp only if I could get a cell phone afterwards—another side benefit."

"Then if that's not the reason, what *was*?"

Amber smiled dreamily. "There was this cute Goth guy in my geometry class last year, and I mean—to-die-for cute, but he never even noticed me. So, I decided to get the piercings and it worked! He talks to me now and everything. He even helped me dye my hair. Our whole group's going to get a tattoo next."

Rinnie understood now, and it made her sad.

The struggling plane passed overhead again. It circled again, dipping dangerously, its wheels brushing the tops of the trees as it flew past.

Rinnie said, "Oh oh, looks like he's coming down. Let's get out of the way."

No sooner had they cleared the center of the lake than Rinnie's prediction came true. The plane skimmed over the trees, abruptly dropping lower and lower, until it came to a sputtering splash.

The girls hung on tight as a wild wave lifted the canoe, followed by cracking sounds and a strange choking roar. The plane tipped backwards, then rocked forward.

"It's gonna go under!" Amber screeched.

"I know! Let's get over there and see if anyone needs help."

The girls paddled as fast as they could to the side of the precariously bobbing aircraft. Amber strained to see inside.

"There's one guy. I can't tell if he's breathing. We need to get closer."

"Okay, but watch that wing. We don't want to go down with it."

"Gotcha!"

They floated in as close as they dared. Amber, barely balancing, peered inside the wreckage. "He's hunched over. There's blood on his face, but he moved a little."

"He's got to get outta there—there's not much time! Whack it!"

"Hey, mister, wake up!" Amber yelled as she bumped the window with her oar.

"Hit it harder!"

"It'll break the window!"

"Who cares?"

"Right." Amber's face set with determination. She yelled between whacks. "Hey you, wake up!"

"Wake up!" Rinnie yelled too.

Amber hit the plane so hard that she nearly fell into the water.

"Careful—careful!" Rinnie warned, and steadied the canoe.

Amber started screaming, "Come on, come on!"

Rinnie joined in. "Come on, come on!"

Finally, the dazed man squinted at them in disbelief.

"No, you're not dreaming. We're real. Wake up. You're sinking—get it? Your plane is sinking. You have to get out—now!"

The man tried to slide toward the door. He didn't get far.

"He's stuck!"

Rinnie's mind whirled. "Wait, wait. Seat belt!"

"Gotcha!" Amber yelled at the man, "Seat belt, seat belt. Undo the seat belt!"

"Seat belt, seat belt," Rinnie chanted loudly.

Soon the man got over to the side and started pushing the door. The plane tipped, and the canoe wobbled sharply.

"Back off, back off!" Rinnie yelled, and they pulled away.

Water poured in as the door began to open. Time was running out. They had to get closer again.

"Go, go!" Amber motioned forward.

They paddled hard. The wing slid perilously close to the canoe. Amber pushed away from it quickly, then reaching out as far as she could, held out the oar for the man to grab. He lunged for it, but missed. The plane slid beneath the surface. The man went with it.

"No!" Both girls screamed.

Bubbles boiled to the surface of the water.

"Can you see him?" Rinnie called out.

"No! Oh—wait. Yes!"

An arm came up out of the water and grabbed the oar. The girls squealed happily.

"Way to go, Amber! Get him to hang onto the side."

Amber did, and the canoe started to swamp.

"Whoa!" Rinnie threw her weight to the other side as fast as she could. "Shift! Lean!" she yelled.

Amber tried to, then cried out, "I can't. I've got to hang on to him. He's too weak."

Rinnie adjusted her weight again, hoping it would be enough to counterbalance.

The confused man lifted his leg to get into the boat.

"Stop!" Both girls screeched.

An air horn blared. Startled, the girls turned to look. The canoe rocked, and the man fell backwards into the water. Gliding up beside him were Sarge and Dad 2.

Amber and Rinnie nearly collapsed with relief, but there was no time to chat. It took several minutes to stabilize the vessels, and provide the support needed so the leaders could maneuver the injured man safely aboard. They wrapped him in a blanket immediately.

A joyous shout came from the observers on the lakeshore. Rinnie and Amber didn't realize they'd had an audience. They were too exhausted to care.

"Let's go, girls. You've got to get to shore," Sarge sternly advised. "We can't do it for you, and the longer you sit there, the harder it'll be. Come on!"

It took all their strength to start paddling again.

Applause erupted when the boats reached the dock. Dad 1 had driven the truck and camper as close to the lake as he safely could. It would serve as an emergency vehicle until they got within cell phone range and could alert the nearest hospital.

Rinnie and Amber were thrilled to be on solid ground again. Their legs wobbled, making it difficult to walk. Cookie and Echo hug-wrapped a blanket around each of them, and took them immediately to the first-aid cabin.

"That was a brave thing you did, girls. But very risky," Echo said, handing them some hot chocolate to sip while they sat on cots to rest.

"Do you th-think he'll be o-k-kay?" Rinnie shivered.

"Don't worry. He'll get the help he needs."

"I couldn't hang onto him. I tried, but I couldn't hang onto him!" Amber cried. "And there was blood running down his face. It was awful!"

Cookie wrapped an arm around Amber's shoulders. "Just breathe slowly now and relax."

"What if they hadn't gotten there? What if they hadn't helped us?" Rinnie moaned. "He would've drowned!"

"Don't what-if yourselves, girls. They got there, that's what counts. It was bad, but thanks to your quick thinking, it wasn't a disaster. There's a lot to be thankful for."

The consoling conversation went on for more than an hour and included a discussion regarding whether they wanted to go home. When that was ruled out, and the girls had unwound enough, they dozed off to sleep.

A timid knock on the first-aid door woke Rinnie. It took her a second to make sense of where she was. Her aching arms brought back the memory of the afternoon's adventure. Lynnette and Kiana tiptoed to the side of her cot.

"Are you guys awake?"

"It's dinnertime. They said we could ask if you were like hungry."

"Who's *they*?" Amber asked, groggily.

The girls all giggled.

Rinnie stretched. "I don't know about you, Amber, but I'm starved!"

"Me too."

"Tell 'em we're on our way."

"Okay, we will." Lynnette hesitated. "But we still like need to ask you something."

"Ask us what?"

"We know you've like had a horrible day and all, but it's Follies night tonight, and we like need to know if our cabin is going to have a skit, or not."

"I figured we'd still help," Rinnie said.

"Unless you don't want us to," Amber shrugged.

"We do!"

"We do!"

"Okay, so I guess we need to eat fast or we won't have time to practice."

Lynnette smiled. "You guys are awesome!"

"You're heroes," Kiana said, then she whispered, "By the way, did you happen to see any underwear lying around today? I'm missing a pair."

Amber giggle-snorted. "What?"

"Sorry," Rinnie grinned. "We've been a little preoccupied."

"It's okay. Just thought I'd ask. See you in a few minutes."

Amber began to put on her shoes. "So, do you feel like a hero?"

"I feel like a hot fudge sundae."

"Seriously."

Rinnie mulled over the question, then said, "My dad says a hero is someone who keeps his wits together and helps when it would be easier to walk away. I guess, with what we did today, we qualify. Does it matter?"

"Not really, but it sure was wild!"

"And scary!"

"Yeah! I'm glad you were the one out there with me."

"Me too. I think you and me are going to be talking about this for a long time."

"For sure!"

Amber turned to Rinnie again as they stepped out onto the porch. "Thanks for coming to find me. I hope you know that I'd never steal stuff. Not shoes, and especially not underwear!"

"Of course I know."

"I haven't been around church much, so they assume I've gone bad."

"Well, I'm gonna tell them to cut it out!"

"Thanks."

"No problem."

A few steps later, Rinnie turned to Amber. "It needs to go both ways."

"What do you mean?"

"I'll tell my friends not to put you down because you don't go to church, if you tell your friends not to put me down because I *do*. Deal?"

"Deal!"

"I guess we get to go rescue the skit now," Rinnie chuckled.

Amber shook her head. "Not on an empty stomach!"

Chapter 20

Fireweed Follies

Lynnette handed out a paper to each with the revamped words to the song, *America the Beautiful.* The group really had to focus.

"I don't like this," Carla grumbled.

"We don't have time to argue about it. Fireweed Follies starts in ninety minutes," Rinnie said, firmly, as she changed shoes. Between the rain on Wednesday and the plane mishap, her sneakers were a sloshy mess. She'd have to wear her heavy hiking boots for the rest of the time at camp. The prospect of that made her just cranky enough that she wasn't about to take garbage from anyone.

"There ought to be something else ..."

"I could tell knot-knot jokes," Amber offered.

"Never mind! Let's get on with it."

Since Lynnette had written most of the skit, she played director.

"Okay, like here's how we need to stand in line for this. First Amber, then Kiana, then me, then Carla, then Rinnie."

"Why does it matter?" Carla groaned.

"It just does. You'll see in a minute," Kiana insisted.

"Here's how it goes." Lynnette sang the first verse. "Camp Kachemak, Camp Kachemak, we sure had lots of fun. We did our chores and ate s'mores, and played out in the sun. Camp Kachemak is just the place for spunky girls like we. Tell Booger bear to stay away from C to shining C.

"Now when we sing *Camp Kachemak*, cross your arms like this over your heart like you mean *love.* When we like sing *chores*, pretend like you're sweeping or chopping wood or something. When we sing the *Booger bear* part, one of the girls on each end will like chase the other one around us once. Who wants to be Booger bear, Amber or Rinnie?"

Amber volunteered. "I'll do it. My hair's darker."

"That's an understatement!" Carla sniggered.

Rinnie almost said something, but Lynnette continued assertively.

"When we sing *from C to shining C*, hold your arms down like a "V" in front of you. Our arms will like cross over each other, and it will look really cool. Be sure to like smile pretty so we'll all look more *shining* than like normal.

"The second verse goes like this: Call, Crowley, Cole, Clupp, Cumberland. Our door said, 'C's the day.' We tried to make the best of things, even a rainy day. Camp Kachemak will soon be just a joyful memory. Our hearts will tug, we send a hug to all this company."

"Good job, you two!" Rinnie said.

"Thank you!" Lynnette said.

Kiana smiled.

Carla groaned again.

Lynnette pressed on. "When we sing our names, point to yourself. Wiggle your fingers like downward to look like rain in that part. Cross your arms again like across your chest for *Camp Kachemak* part, and do it again for the *our hearts will tug* part, and then unfold your arms and hold them straight out in front of you like you're reaching out to hug the audience."

"This is too complicated!"

Lynnette stomped her foot. "Okay, who votes to like get busy and practice this?"

Four raised their hands.

"Okay, who votes to have like nothing prepared and look like total fools?"

Carla made no comment. The practice could continue.

The skit turned out alright, considering how fast they'd put it together. The audience really got a kick out of the Booger bear part because Rinnie squealed like a ninny as she ran, and Amber hammed up the growling.

Jessica's cabin had the best skit. It was about friendship. They had cute dialogue, and ended by singing, *Anytime You Need a Friend*, by Mariah Carey. Two girls took turns on the solo parts, and they were fantastic. The other girls were perfect backup singers. They'd practiced a lot, and it showed. Their actions were in sync, and Jessica was even participating. Before the skit was over the audience was singing and swaying along.

Rinnie knew this was a huge leap for Jessica, and the fact that she was wearing the T-shirt Rinnie had given her made it even neater. She was glad that Jessica had been placed in a cabin like that. There was too much drama trauma going on in cabin C!

After campfire, the leaders asked to talk to Amber again. She consented reluctantly, but when she came back to the cabin she appeared to be pleased.

"You okay?" Rinnie asked.

"Yup."

Carla was upset. "I don't know what you two think is so okay. My shoes are still missing and no one mentioned anything about it at campfire tonight."

"That's because I told them what I've been telling you all week," Kiana reported. "On Monday, after volleyball, you tied the laces together and hung the shoes on a bush to dry in the sun. A squirrel family has probably made a new home in them and is using my missing underwear for a blanket."

Carla glared at her. "You're pathetic."

Kiana glared back. "So? There are worse things to be."

101

Chapter 21

Early-Morning Mayhem

"Get up, slackers!" Carla demanded. "It's our turn to help with breakfast. Cookie and Lynnette are already out there."

Rinnie lifted her head groggily. "Be there in a minute. You go ahead."

"No way. I'm gonna make sure you're awake so I don't get stuck with all the work—again. Up, up, up!"

"Cut it out! We heard the first time you barked," Amber complained.

Carla shook the bottom bunk hard. "Come on, you too, Kiana," she growled.

Rinnie spoke up defensively. "Leave her alone. We'll be there in a minute—I promise. Just go!"

Carla paused. "Okay, but hurry. The cabin F girls are already at the flagpole."

"That's nothing new. They're always the first ones there."

"I know, but there's something you won't want to miss." Carla snickered as she was leaving.

"What's she up to now?" Kiana yawned.

"I don't know," Rinnie answered, as she slowly slid off her bunk. "But if she's happy about it, it can't be good."

"That's for sure. We'd better get out there." Amber murmured. "I hope it's warmer today. I'm tired of wearing cold, damp clothes."

Kiana giggled. "At least you can find all of yours."

As the cabin C stragglers made their way across camp,

Rinnie took in a deep breath of the exhilarating fresh air. "Ooh, I love the smell of mountains in the morning, and listen to the birds!"

"Watch out, she's gonna start singing *The Sound of Music*." Amber joked.

Rinnie smiled. "You could join me."

"Later. For now let's enjoy the moment—in silence."

Kiana sighed. "I like how everything is so peaceful."

"It's a little too peaceful," Amber noted suspiciously, as the three neared the flagpole.

The cabin F girls whispered amongst themselves and glanced frequently in Kiana's direction. Some were apprehensive. Some were amused. Carla stood a short distance away, an impish grin on her face.

"What the …?" Amber said.

"Oh, no!" Rinnie said.

Kiana stared upward, horrified.

Something bizarre hung from the flagpole. It wasn't red, white, and blue. It was red, white, and black—a pair of large panties with the words "Kiana's Wide Load" written in bold markers.

"I guess squirrels didn't steal them after all," Carla smirked, then doubled over with laughter.

Kiana's lips quivered. She looked at all the faces awaiting her reaction. Her breathing came in gasps. Pale and unsteady, she turned and clumsily ran for the cabin.

Rinnie and Amber were flabbergasted. They stormed the flagpole and tore down the display.

"Carla, you're a jerk!" Rinnie fumed.

"A spiteful, snotty, spoiled jerk!" Amber seethed.

"I am not! It's not my fault you guys don't have a sense of humor."

Amber rolled the panties up in her fist. "Come here. I'll show you humor."

Carla began backing down the field.

"I've got this one, Rinnie. You take Kiana."

"I'm on it."

Carla started running. "Cookie! Help!" she screamed.

Kiana was lying face down in her pillow, sobbing.

Rinnie wanted to furiously vent a ton of pent-up Carla frustrations, but realized that what Kiana needed was calm comfort.

"I c-could die," Kiana forced out between gasps.

Carefully Rinnie stroked her head. "Don't say that. You can't let her win," she coaxed.

Kiana broke down again.

Surely, Cookie would come to check on things soon, Rinnie thought. She anxiously watched the window, as though watching and wishing would get the leader there faster.

A reckoning took place inside cabin C before anything else that morning. The rest of the leaders congregated on the porch waiting for Cookie and Echo to come out. Rinnie, Amber, and Lynnette were a few feet away straining their ears to hear what was being said. Before long, Carla appeared in the doorway with her clothes, sleeping bag, and backpack.

"Take this girl to the pavilion," Echo instructed Sarge. "She's lost her camp privileges." She turned to Carla. "You'd be headed home right now if camp wasn't over tomorrow, and if Kiana wasn't so forgiving. I suggest you contemplate your unkind actions. You'll do nothing but kitchen duty for the rest of your time here."

Carla didn't look at the other girls as she walked by. All the leaders left except Cookie, who was still chatting with Kiana. Rinnie ran back inside to join them.

"I'm sorry that things have been so rough with Carla. Usually I just fix the food and don't interact much with the girls. This year I wanted to be more involved. But I should've paid closer attention."

Rinnie disagreed. "It's not your fault, Cookie. She's impossible to deal with!"

"I know."

Kiana quit biting the side of her finger and said, "I'm going to stay away from her. She doesn't like me."

"You won't always like every person you meet. The trick is to not let them know it. It's a sign of grace and maturity."

"That lets me out," Rinnie said. "I think Carla knows she's not my favorite person.

"She probably has no clue."

"She sure likes to talk about ghosts a lot. Do you believe in ghosts, Cookie?"

"Kiana, honey, this is how I feel about them. They might exist. But the good ones probably have important stuff to do, and I need to stay out of their way. And if there are bad ones, they'd better stay out of *my* way! There are so many *living* souls, who need food, or shelter, or tender loving care that I don't have time to be worrying over mischievous dead ones. It's a waste of time!"

Rinnie grinned, "Not much scares you, I bet."

"To tell you the truth, what scares me the most is when I see people doing mean, rotten things, when they know better. It sure makes the world a harder place to live in."

Kiana sighed. "This day is crazy already, and we haven't even had breakfast yet!"

Cookie gasped, "Oh, dear, I've gotta get back to work!"

Chapter 22

Sisters at Heart

It was Rinnie's turn to sweep out the cabin. She was glad for some extra time alone to think. What could she give Jessica for the last secret-sister gift?

The day before, Rinnie had received a pair of socks with multi-colored toes from her secret sister. It came with a note that read, "May you run and not be weary; walk and not faint; and may your feet stay warm while you're at it." It was clever. But once more, she couldn't run the risk of possibly giving them back to the person who had given them to her, so that option was out.

She considered scrubbing the blue off the hugging angels statue, but not for long. It was desperation not inspiration, and there was no way it would've worked. Rinnie had to face the obvious. There was only one other option—her much-loved triple-heart necklace.

But how could she possibly give that necklace away? Her stomach twisted. How could she not? The sweeping stopped. Rinnie tore another piece of paper from her journal and made a card. That done, she ran as fast as she could to Cabin E, and when no one was looking, carefully placed the precious gift in Jessica Jeffries' mailbox.

When Rinnie checked her own mailbox later, there was a tiny looking glass with flower-shaped beads around the edge of the mirror, and a note that read: "You are someone I ad-mirror!" It was so corny that she couldn't help but smile. She couldn't look at her reflection long though without getting tearful.

During free time on Friday afternoon Rinnie headed for Ponder Rock with her new notebook and pen. There was a crispness to the breeze and she wanted to sit on the big warm rock and relax. A handful of girls had already gathered out there. Jessica was one of them. She wasn't saying much, just standing around, listening—and wearing the necklace.

Rinnie felt a twinge of remorse when she saw it. Maybe she could buy another necklace when they got back into town and see if Jessica would trade back. No, she knew that wasn't right. She'd made a choice and would have to live with it, but it wasn't easy.

Rinnie found a place to sit, and joined in the chatter.

Eventually, the other girls left and Jessica asked, "Do you mind if I still sit here?"

"Heck no! Have a seat."

There was an awkward silence. Rinnie wasn't sure what to say.

Jessica took an envelope out of her pocket and sat looking at it.

"The letter-from-home thing was one of the things I liked most about camp. My mom sent me an awesome card." As soon as she said it, Rinnie was sorry she had. Obviously Jessica's letter wouldn't be from her mom, duh!

Thankfully, Jessica didn't react as though Rinnie had been insensitive. She just looked down and said, "Yeah."

There was another awkward silence. Rinnie pretended to be glancing intently through her notebook, which was difficult because nothing had been written in it yet.

A few minutes later, Jessica looked up and asked, "Do you know why I moved to Alaska?"

"I heard something about it."

"Then you guessed that my letter was from my aunt, not my mom."

Rinnie could see tears in Jessica's eyes. "Your aunt's super. She's good friends with my mom."

"Yeah, I know. She told me to find you here if I felt like talking. She said you were cool."

"Oh, gee, that was nice of her to say."

"Yeah, she's real nice. She's having a hard time too, ya know, because my mom was her only sister and all. My uncle's nice too. It's just not the same."

"I bet."

Jessica took a deep breath and blurted out, "My folks were killed by a drunk driver. The guy had been arrested so many times that he didn't even have a license anymore. I still can't believe it. I mean, how can that happen?" Jessica sobbed.

Rinnie didn't know how to answer, so she just listened. It was hard for her not to cry too.

Jessica slowly wiped her eyes, sniffled, and put the letter in her pocket. "Alaska feels so different to me. I'm used to a big city and people everywhere. Here it's so spread out and has all this wildlife to worry about."

"There aren't any muggers," Rinnie teased.

"True, but nobody ever had to warn me that the mugger might eat me."

"True," Rinnie chuckled.

"I was worried about coming to camp."

"I'm glad you came."

"It took me a while, but I'm glad too—especially today. I got the best present from my secret sister. It's helped me a lot."

Rinnie gulped. "R-really? What was it?"

Jessica lifted up the necklace. "See?"

"That's c-cool." Rinnie struggled to get the words out.

"It helped me remember a couple of things. It's like I'm the heart in the middle, and no matter where they are, my mom and dad are next to me. They will always be close to my heart." Jessica swallowed hard. "And this afternoon I realized that I can look at it another way—that I have two sets of parents now. One on each side of me, and I don't have to choose between them. They all love me." She paused for a moment, then continued. "I think I'm going to be okay. This necklace will help give me courage to go forward."

All Rinnie could do was smile.

Crossing the field with a group, Amber hollered out, "Hey, you two. Come and go swimming with us."

"No thanks, I'm working on my tan."

"Oh, come on, Rinnie. I promise not to dunk ya."

"As if!"

Amber laughed and waved.

Jessica wiped her eyes again. "She's *so* funny."

"She sure is!"

"So, do you want to go to the lake?"

"Me? No. I had enough water excitement yesterday."

"That was really great what you guys did."

"Thanks. It was pretty intense."

Jessica hesitated. "If you don't care, maybe I'll go with them. Okay?"

"Sure—no problem."

"Thanks for listening."

"Anytime. I'm thinking about getting a group together for lunch at the mall before school starts."

"That'd be cool!" Jessica said, and ran to catch up with Amber and the others.

Finally, Rinnie had had a chance to get to know her secret sister. It was a good beginning. Poor kid—what a harsh thing to happen to someone—no wonder she was shy.

Rinnie was ashamed. She'd been so wrapped up in herself. What if she hadn't bothered to find out Jessica's story—figured she was weird and ignored her? What if she'd been selfish and held back on the necklace? She pondered that for a while.

Chapter 23

Daydream Danger

Ponder Rock had one particularly smooth groove on it and, if Rinnie sat just so, it worked like a recliner with a place to lean back slightly and a flatter place to stretch out her legs. From this vantage point she could see girls playing in the lake, leaders chatting near the cabins, and Cookie fixing the last big meal of camp. Carla had been helping her all day and looked miserable.

In this atmosphere, Rinnie mulled over what to put in the new notebook. Should she write about what had happened with Jessica? No, she'd put that in her journal. She wanted this notebook to be imaginative. One day she hoped to write a book. She loved the possibility of someday seeing her own book on library shelves.

Rinnie opened the notebook and daydreamed as she flipped through the fresh, clean pages. She was glad to be going home soon. Her house might be old, but her room was bigger than the whole cabin she'd spent the week in. How did the early settlers ever live in such tiny cabins?

An interesting notion came to Rinnie. She liked to read about the early days on the Alaska frontier, so why not write about it? Okay. Now where would the setting be? In one of those towns where people got horribly sick and medicine had to be brought in by dogsled to save them? That might work, but she'd need to research for details. In the meantime she could work on other parts of the story. She would write about a girl her age. Hmm, what would the girl's name be?

Cilla. Hmm, where'd that come from? She'd never heard

that name before. Cilla—like short for Priscilla? Rinnie was short for Lorinda, so why not? With that decision made, Rinnie commenced.

It was a dark and dreary, stormy winter's night. Cilla was worn out. Everybody in her family was sick—her mom, her brothers—even their dog, and she had to take care of them.

Rinnie chewed on her pen cap briefly, and changed her mind. She crossed out the dark dreary stormy part, and began again.

The girls returned from the lake and were getting ready for dinner. The leaders were helping Cookie. Rinnie's dad had arrived early to help load the trailer. He was talking to others at the pavilion. But Rinnie had lost track of time and hadn't even noticed.

When she was at the part where the girl left the cabin to get wood from the shed, and had written, *Cilla heard a noise behind her. It was a swishing sound—like something coming through the tall brush behind her*, Rinnie stopped. That wouldn't work. It'd be frozen out there. Cilla wouldn't have heard the brush swishing. But Rinnie had heard it, was still hearing it—and it was coming from directly behind *her.*

"Come on you guys, you can't scare me," she challenged, expecting Amber to jump out of the bushes. Instead of that, Rinnie heard heavy breathing. It reminded her of the low huffing sound made by the huge black bear at the Anchorage zoo as he paced in his pen, gazing up at the tourists as though they were tasty morsels.

Rinnie's heart beat faster. What was she supposed to do? All the bear-fact lectures she'd ever heard became jumbled in her mind. *Don't go off on your own.* There was a whole field between her and the leaders at the pavilion. Technically, she was off on her own, away from the group. Not good, not good! *You can't outrun a bear.* Rinnie didn't know how close the predator was. She groaned, "Get large and loud—and hope somebody notices!"

The notebook and pen tumbled onto the ground as Rinnie stood up on the rock and turned to face the beast. At the same

111

time, about a hundred feet away, the bear stood up on its hind legs to get a better view of his prey. He was six feet tall.

Rinnie forced the lump in her throat downward as she tried to gruffly yell, "Hey, bear!" It sounded like a gagging reflex.

The Alaska flag song popped into her head. Rinnie didn't have time to think about how weird that was—she just started singing. The first notes sounded more like a squawk than song, but she didn't care. She sang louder. "Eight stars of gold on a field of blue. Alaska's flag may it mean to you, the blue of the sea, the evening sky …"

The bear wasn't scared off by her singing and started moving toward her again.

"Get! Go away! Leave!" she yelled, hoarsely, waving her arms above her head. She needed something to throw. A pen? Like that would do any good.

The bear kept coming—steadily forward.

Rinnie tried yelling again, her voice a bit stronger. "Shoo, you rotten snot, you Booger bear. Shoo!" Suddenly an idea came to her. Don't shoo him, shoe him! Yes, that's something she could throw. Rinnie struggled to take her left hiking boot off and loosened the laces on the right one while she was at it. She had only two chances. She had to make each shot count.

The bear, at thirty feet, was too far away. He had to be closer, and he was getting closer by the second. Rinnie took aim and let it rip!

Plunk! The boot fell about a yard in front of the bear. The beast sniffed and chewed on it for a moment, then resumed its course—in Rinnie's direction.

"Dang it! I *do* throw like a girl!" Rinnie despaired. The yelling and singing hadn't worked. The shoe shooing had flopped. Now what? A combination of the three? It was worth a try. Rinnie began singing faster as she struggled to take off the last boot.

"Eight stars of gold on a field of blue. Alaska's flag may it mean to you, the blue of the sea, the evening sky, the mountain lakes and the flow'rs nearby." Over her shoulder she called out, "Hello, I'm not doing this for fun, people. I could use some help here!" Rinnie took aim again. "The gold of the early Sourdough dreams, the precious gold of the hills and streams …"

Carla looked up from setting tables to see who was torturing the flag song. "Look! Booger's getting Rinnie!" she pointed excitedly, just as Rinnie launched the hiking boot as hard as she could, and hollered, "Get your fuzzy face out of here, hairball!"

Chaos followed.

The leaders shouted at the girls to run for the cabins. They screamed and scrambled.

Cookie grabbed two pots and began clanging them together. The dads came running across the field with their pistols drawn. Rinnie's dad outran them all.

However, by the time they got to Ponder Rock, Booger the bear was halfway to Canada. Rinnie's throw had nailed him right on the snout. A week's worth of frustration came pouring out. She began whooping and squealing, "Alright! Girls can throw. Bears can go! Girls can throw. Bears can go! Alright! Alright! Alright!"

"Rinnie, Rinnie, it's okay! He's gone!"

She spun around. Dad? Was she dreaming? No, she couldn't be.

"Did you see that, Dad? Did you see?"

"Yeah, it was great. Now, here, let me help you down."

Rinnie practically flew into his arms. She was ready for one of those big dad-hugs, and she got it.

Chapter 24

The Last Campfire

At campfire that night Rinnie sat by her dad wrapped in a blanket, drinking hot chocolate. It wasn't a cold night, but Rinnie was shaky and her energy reserves were low.

The leaders took turns talking about how terrific the week had been, and gave out awards. The cabin awards came first. The Cleanest Cabin Award went to the Cabin D girls. They'd passed the daily inspections four out of four times, and Echo made a point of noting, "There wasn't a mouse dropping, cobweb or beetle carcass ever to be found. The shoes were also lined up perfectly every day, and were never muddy—even after the rainstorm."

"Sounds like some girls need to get out more," Rinnie's dad whispered.

A giggle-snort nearly sent hot chocolate spurting from Rinnie's nose.

Best Skit was a no-brainer. Cabin E won. There was lots of applause. "C's the day!" got Rinnie's group an award for Best Door Theme. Lynnette accepted graciously. Cabin A's glittered handprints won Best Window Decoration. Sprucing up their porch with pine cones won Cabin B an award for Most Organic Décor. Always-early Cabin F got the Rise and Shine Award.

Each girl received recognition for something. Efforts had been noticed—even trivial ones. There were activity awards for hiking, swimming, and so forth. Skills awards included things like Best Hot Dog Stick whittled during knife safety class. A First Aid award went to the girl who'd correctly bandaged the finger of the girl who'd whittled the best hot dog stick.

Amber won the Best Knot Tying award for her efforts in class and for teaching other girls how to make knotty necklaces afterwards. Kiana won an award for First Marshmallow Cooked over Best Fire Started. Lynnette received the craft class award for Happiest Helper. She'd often stayed behind to put away supplies. Carla's recognition was for being the Most Prepared because she'd had an extra pair of socks on the hike.

If Rinnie had designed an award for herself, it would have been something like Dirtiest Hair, or Most Gullible for getting caught up in all the ghost story business, but instead she received the Beary Brave award. That was nice.

"Am I supposed to share this with Booger or will he get a copy in the mail?" she asked, when she went up to receive the scroll of paper.

People chuckled, and her dad gave her a high five when she got back to her seat.

The Juls got a Super Service Award along with the leaders and the camp dads.

Echo made an announcement at that point. "I wanted to tell you that we received word this evening that Mr. Myers—the gentleman who was helped out of the lake yesterday—is doing well. At this time, we'd like to present Amber Call and Rinnie Cumberland with the Just Plane Wonderful award."

Everyone clapped.

The last award was called the Forget-Me-Not Award. It usually went to the person who'd blossomed at camp. This year that award went to Jessica Jeffries. Everyone cheered.

With that, the Camp Kachemak Awards Ceremony was finished, and the Juls gathered to sing a song they'd put together. It went something like:

I'm going back, going back, going back
To Camp Kachemak, Kachemak, Kachemak

I wanna sleep in a sack in a shack,
And eat s'mores for a snack, for a snack, for a snack.
Mean mosquitoes I'll whack, yes I'll whack, yes I'll whack
The ones I miss I will scratch, I will scratch, I will scratch.
The smell of pine and Calamine make me wanna go back,
to Camp Kachemak.

There was a second verse, but Rinnie missed it because her dad leaned down and said, "Mom said to give you a big hug. The boys said you should hurry home. They're tired of doing all the dishes. Rascal thinks he owns your bed now, so that might be a problem. Nick hasn't been hanging out around our house this week. I saw him in the store. His mom arrived earlier than expected so they were buying a bunch of groceries. He said to tell you hi."

Nick hadn't been over to hang out with Squid? Hmm. Was it because his mom was in town, or because Rinnie wasn't home? Was he still *her* friend after all? Interesting questions. She could hardly wait to discover the answers.

During the last part of the campfire, they went around the circle and every girl who wanted to tell what she'd enjoyed the most that week was given one minute to do so. Some comments were comical. Others were emotional. Camp Kachemak, for the most part, had been a success. No one mentioned anything unpleasant. Good idea, Rinnie thought. Move through it and move on.

It was nearly 11 p.m. when the Juls led everyone in songs one more time, and Echo made her final announcement.

"Thank you, everyone for making this a memorable experience. There are no more marshmallows, so we'll dispense with s'mores making tonight."

That was fine with Rinnie. She'd eaten enough s'mores to last her for a year!

Echo continued. "Don't stay up all night packing. Get some sleep. You'll have plenty of time in the morning.

Remember to drop off all your gear at the big trailer *before* heading to breakfast."

The girls grumbled.

"I know, I know. But we've found that people pack faster when they're hungry. And after breakfast, check the cleanup charts that'll be posted at the pavilion. We need to get this place spiffed up. There's another group scheduled for Camp Kachemak next week so we can't leave a mess. Work together. We'd like to get on the road for home by ten. Thank you all again, and good night."

———

Standing in line at the porta-potties gave Rinnie a moment to reflect. This year's camp wasn't perfect, but it hadn't been a total disaster. She'd reestablished the friendship with Amber, and gotten to know Kiana better. Lynnette was neat too, but it was obvious they'd never again be as close as they'd been in elementary school. Still, Rinnie knew that in a pinch, she and Lynnette would be there for each other.

Then there was Carla. She sure got people going. Rinnie wouldn't miss Carla, and she felt bad about that—sort of. But like Cookie said, "You won't always like every person that you meet. The trick is to not let them know it." Had Rinnie failed with Carla? Probably. But as long as Rinnie had a brother Carla had a crush on, there'd be plenty of opportunities to try again. As a matter of fact, another chance was already on the horizon. Carla had made her promise four times to tell J.R. how she'd saved Rinnie from the bear.

———

As she gathered her clothes before bed, Rinnie realized the challenge would be to get everything back *into* the duffle bag. Before camp everything had been carefully folded and stacked. Now it was every shirt for itself in the sock-eat-sock world of dirty camp clothes. Rinnie was about to separate what few clean clothes were left over from all the dirty ones, but soon realized it was useless. Everything needed to be washed. If it wasn't dirty, it was smoky, or sticky from people bumping into her with marshmallows.

Rinnie checked her camera. There were a few pictures left. "Hey, look up!"

Kiana did and Rinnie took her picture.

"Now I see spots. Whee!"

"Sorry!" Rinnie apologized.

"It's okay. Can I get a copy of those?"

"Sure. It may take me a week or two to get 'em developed. I used all my babysitting money before camp."

"I hear ya! I can help pay if you let me know how much."

"Okey dokey."

Kiana hesitated. "Rinnie, I wanted to say that I'm really glad you were my bunkmate."

"Me too."

"It was sweet when you patted my head," Kiana teased.

"Ha ha! I hope you remember it, because it won't happen again!"

They could laugh about some of the morning's mayhem, but avoided talking about the traumatic part. Thankfully the leaders had stuck to their word. Carla wasn't allowed back into their cabin. Rinnie was glad. She couldn't stand another ghost story argument.

"Now I want to tell you something," Rinnie said. "By the end of the week when you were standing up for yourself and others, I was proud of you! You need to keep it up."

"I'll try." Kiana smiled.

"You better. By the way, some of us are gonna get together for lunch at the mall before school starts. You should come."

Kiana was pleasantly surprised. "That'd be way cool."

"I'll call you when we get the details figured out. I want Erica to come too."

"Didn't you hear? They're moving."

Rinnie's smile disappeared. "What?"

"Yeah, that's what part of their trip was about. Sorry, I thought you knew."

"No." Rinnie's limited energy evaporated. Her shoulders sagged.

Kiana tried to comfort her. "It's gonna be hard with Erica moving and all, but we can stick together."

Rinnie nodded slightly.

Lynnette came back into the cabin, she headed for bed immediately. "I can't like stay up and chat," she apologized. "My family's like leaving for Valdez as soon as I get home and I don't want to be like wasted."

In a soft voice, Rinnie said, "No problem. Hope you have a nice trip. Thanks for pulling the skit together. It was fun."

"You're welcome. I appreciate your support." Lynnette thanked Kiana for her help too then curled up in her bag and was asleep in a flash.

Rinnie wasn't far behind. She couldn't even remember hearing Amber or Cookie come into the cabin.

Chapter 25

Parting Shots

Rinnie Cumberland was running, running, running. She could barely breathe! Someone was chasing her, gaining on her. Who was it? Who? She glanced behind. There was mean, haggy Magda riding in an airplane with Booger the bear swooping down on Rinnie, who was in a canoe in the middle of the lake without a paddle. Meanwhile, Carla stood on the shore with a blue ribbon in her hair and honked.

Honked?

Rinnie's nightmare faded when the second air horn sounded. Quaking, she rolled out of her sleeping bag and joined the flurry of activity that was typical for a Saturday morning at camp. Because of the new rule—the first ones packed were the first ones to eat—the place resembled a beehive. People darted in and out of cabins. As quickly as possible, girls and leaders dropped their belongings off at the long trailer and made a beeline for the breakfast buffet. Rinnie was the last one out of cabin C. Amber was waiting on the porch.

"Hey! Glad to see somebody waited. I was afraid I'd been abandoned."

"You almost were," Amber razzed. "Didn't think you'd ever wake up!"

They dropped their stuff off at the trailer and headed across the field to the pavilion.

"So, you're riding home with your dad?"

"Yeah, sorry. Hope you don't feel deserted."

"Me? Nah. I'll sit up front and talk to Cookie."

"Good plan."

They walked in silence for a few steps, then Amber stopped. "I have a confession to make."

"About what?"

"It was me."

Rinnie's mind reeled. Oh no! Had Amber taken Carla's shoes after all? Rinnie nervously asked, "What was?"

"I was your secret sister."

Rinnie was so relieved! "Really? Wow, that's so cool—thanks!"

"Okay … that was more excitement than I imagined, but hey, you're welcome," Amber kidded. Then she took a deep breath. "While we're at it, thanks from me too."

"From you?"

Amber choked back emotion. "Yeah. You don't know this, but I saw what you were going through—that your secret-sister stuff was ruined. I was watching how you'd deal with it, and wondering if you'd give my gifts away. You never did. That meant a lot to me." A tear ran down her cheek.

Rinnie tried not to cry, but she couldn't help it. Naturally a hug had to come next.

Several sniffles later, Amber continued. "I saw what you did with your necklace. I really wanted to make a knotty one for you, to help you not feel so bad. But that would've given my identity away, so I owe you one."

"Thanks. I really like the ones with the beads."

"Me too. Heck, I may go into business."

"You should!"

"But first," Amber held up a wet, streaked hand, "I need a Kleenex."

Rinnie flinched. "Ooh, gross!"

They ran to the porta potties for tissue, and before long were happily chatting away again as they stood in line for food.

"We're going to get together again, right?" Amber asked.

"Absolutely! We'll do something before school starts. I'm thinking we could ask Lynnette and Kiana to come, and that new girl, Jessica."

"Cool! You can invite Carla too, but she won't come if I'm there. I'm not exactly her new best friend. When I said 'buh bye' to her this morning, she stomped off."

"Because you said, 'Buh bye?'"

"Possibly because I also said, 'Try not to get lost on your way home from the outhouse.'"

Rinnie grinned. "Yeah, that's probably why. We'd better let her chill a while. But we can get together with the others."

"And before that, if you want to, you and I can hang out at my house and we'll dye your hair like mine, and I'll introduce you to one of the guys in my group."

"Or not," Rinnie laughed. "But thanks for the offer. I think we should settle for a movie at the mall."

Amber made one of those from-my-eyes-to-yours gestures and said, "Deal! I'll call you on my new cell phone!"

After breakfast, each cabin sent one girl back to sweep and check for clutter. There were plenty of other chores to go around too, like taking down the volleyball net, finding the volleyball, gathering the life jackets, and cleaning several areas. Sarge supervised the portage of the canoes up from the lake which took two groups of five girls each. Cookie got help from three of the Juls to pack up the cooking area. The other three helped to clean out the supply cabin.

Rinnie's group was on fire pit and litter detail. "I choose the fire pit," she said, and grabbed a shovel to stir down the embers. No one else wanted the smoky job, so it worked out. It also gave her an opportunity, between stirring through the ashes, to take pictures of the camp in action.

She got a neat picture of her dad as he helped get all the gear loaded up and ready for the trip back to town. He was such a great guy!

Rinnie also got one of all the grimacing girls who were straining to drag canoes up from the lake.

She captured Carla searching through a patch of prickly devils club for her shoes. Someone had mentioned seeing something pink in that area. Rinnie took a picture of that mischievous someone who chatted innocently with Kiana as they slowly walked around, occasionally picking up scraps of paper. Oh, Amber!

Rinnie had five pictures left on her roll of film when Jessica came up beside her.

"Say cheese!"

"Hi—uh—cheese."

Rinnie snapped a photo. "So, how's it going?"

"It's going."

"Good."

Jessica fidgeted. "I—um—I found out this morning that you're my secret sister and I wanted to say thanks."

"Oh—uh—hey, you're welcome. Who told you it was me?"

"A girl named Carla hinted around about it, and I figured out the rest."

"I'm not surprised," Rinnie said. "Hope it was okay."

"Okay? It was wonderful. It helped me a lot!" She reached up to the triple-heart necklace and started to take it off. "You'll want this back. It was really cool to be able to wear it for a while, but it's probably special to you, and you should take it home."

Rinnie stopped Jessica from undoing the clasp. "Yeah, it *is* special. But it has a new home now."

Jessica smiled through tears, and ran off to help with canoes.

A wonderful feeling flooded over Rinnie. She knew it was the right thing to do. But still, she sniffled a few times while she dumped water onto the last embers of a smoldering log.

After she put the ashes in a previously dug hole and covered them with dirt, Rinnie put the shovel by the tree next to the trailer and helped her dad finish loading. She was glad to be traveling home with him.

When all tasks were completed, Echo called for the group to assemble one last time around the fire pit. "I want to thank everyone again for making our Camp Kachemak experience a memorable one. While you're waiting for your ride home from the church, make sure you gather all your belongings, especially your muddy clothes. I'm not gonna wash them for you. I've got enough of my own to worry about!" Echo chuckled and held up a small box, "One more thing, those who donated their cell phones or CD players to my collection last Monday, can pick them up as soon as we're finished here. Again, thanks to the other leaders and camp dads. I've asked Cookie to offer a prayer for safe travel."

All quieted down. However, before Cookie could begin, a wave of whispers and giggles washed through the group. Rinnie worked her way to the outside of the crowd to see what was up.

Slowly plodding along as it walked across the far corner of the field, was an old bull moose. It had seen better days, and had battle scars on its hide. But it wasn't the scars that had caught everyone's attention. It was an odd flash of pink that swung by its head every few steps.

"What is it?" Rinnie asked Kiana, who looked like a kid at Christmas.

"Watch, when it turns!"

Dad 2 made a moose call and the animal paused to look in their direction.

"Oh my word! Ranger Dan was right. All kinds of things *do* get caught on those big antlers of theirs," Rinnie grabbed her camera. This was one picture she *had* to have. It was too funny!

Dangling from the moose's antlers was a tangled pair of pink sneakers.

Carla stood speechless. Rinnie's camera clicked, then clicked again. Amber's face was aglow with a victorious grin.

Laughter of the Loons

Last in a long line of vehicles, Rinnie and her dad waited for their turn to drive down the packed-gravel road that led out onto the highway.

"Glad to be going home?" he asked.

"Oh—big time! Camping sure makes you appreciate things like shampoo, and showers, and clean clothes, and toilets!"

Her dad nodded. "I don't care what they say, even the most diehard, rough-it camper can't wait to get back to a civilized bathroom."

"I couldn't take rougher than this," Rinnie moaned, and leaned her weary head against the window

The lineup of vehicles began to move forward.

Suddenly Rinnie sat up straight. "Oh—wait. Did you get the shovel by the tree? I left it there by the stuff you were loading."

"A shovel? No, I didn't load a shovel. Guess we're gonna have to go back."

"I can run and get it."

"You sure?"

"No problem," Rinnie said. She was halfway out the door by the time he'd completely stopped.

It was a longer jog than she had figured, though, and she was out of breath when she finally reached the tree. The shovel was right where she'd left it. Rinnie grabbed it and started walking back.

Camp Kachemak looked like an Alaska postcard with its rustic old cabins, framed with wildflowers, birch, and pine trees, nestled near a teal blue lake. A spectacular backdrop of distant mountains, crowned with a touch of snow on the highest peaks, completed the picture-perfect view. Rinnie couldn't resist taking another picture.

Abuzz with activity earlier, the campground felt desolate now. The stillness was uncanny. As she tucked the camera into her jacket pocket, she heard the cry of the loons and turned to see if she could spot them.

The shovel fell to the ground. Rinnie froze in her tracks.

A light blue ribbon waved in the breeze as it fluttered on a bush by the lake. Tiny hairs stood up on the back of Rinnie's neck. Goose bumps followed on her arms and legs. Was she seeing things? She blinked and looked again. Whoa! A gust of wind made the bush sway eerily. The ribbon seemed to dance. She couldn't believe it, and neither would anyone else—not without proof.

Rinnie reached down to grab the camera. Her hands trembled with excitement. She might actually solve the mystery of the lost girl once and for all. The loons called again from the lake. It sounded like laughter. Were they mocking her—or was the laughter coming from *someone else*? Rinnie's heart beat faster. Her fingers fumbled, and the camera twisted up in the pocket lining. She jerked and jerked until it came loose.

The sound of ripping fabric brought Rinnie to her senses. "This is ridiculous. I don't even have the picture yet and I'm already a nervous wreck!" She rationalized, somebody put that ribbon out there—Amber probably, or even Carla for that matter. It was a hoax. It had to be, and she wasn't going to fall for it. Determined, Rinnie turned to leave.

Again the thought of that ribbon teased at her. Having a picture of it would be awesome. What if she managed to get a ghostly image on film? Carla would be so jealous! Rinnie reconsidered. Fine, she'd go for it. There was only one photograph left. She focused the lens carefully—very carefully—and tried not to jiggle. She started to push the button …

Rinnie's dad tapped the horn.

The noise jolted Rinnie. She cried out and jumped. The camera flew out of her hands, and landed on the ground with a mighty thud.

"Are you okay?" he called out the window.

Rinnie's heart was pounding. "Yeah—h-hang on. I'll be r-right th-there!" she stammered. Shaking, she picked up the camera and brushed off the dirt and grass. The film wasn't ruined. Phew! she sighed. Then she took a deep, calming breath of the sweet Alaska air.

That's when Rinnie Cumberland figured out exactly what to do about the eerie feelings, the blue ribbon on the bush, and the spooky camp story. As soon as she decided, the goose bumps disappeared.

Rinnie didn't take a picture. She didn't even try. She simply waved at the bush, and said, "Sorry, my life is complicated enough. See you next year!"

With that, she picked up the shovel and ran to the car without ever looking back.

Other Books by Halene Dahlstrom

Raven Cove Mystery: ISBN 1-59433-001-8
Thirteen-year-old Rinnie Cumberland wasn't afraid to sleep in her brother's old tree house; maybe she should have been. A cry for help plunged Rinnie right into the middle of the *Raven Cove Mystery*.

Christmas Connections: ISBN 1-888125-70-5
Christmas Connections is the tender story of two anxious sisters: one in heaven longing for a name and family, and Suzannah on earth trying to keep her family together.

Harvest Homecoming: ISBN 1-59433-017-4
For 16-year-old, Suzannah Brown, Homecoming was the threshold of her entire high school experience—first big football game—first big dance—first big date. Suzannah couldn't wait!

Coming Soon
The Very Best Thing for TJ, an Adoption Option Story

Halene Dahlstrom

Available for book signings, to speak to schools, clubs, and other organizations. email: author@booksbyhalene.com

Kindly Send Orders To Publication Consultants
8370 Eleusis Drive, Anchorage, AK 99502
(907) 349-2424 Fax (907) 349-2426
www.publicationconsultants.com — books@publicationconsultants.com